Praise for the

# DAUGHTER

series

"A beautifully written dystopian that has you chasing resolution and begging for the happy ending Daughter4254 desperately deserves."

—Jennifer Jenkins, *Nameless* author/
Teen Author Boot Camp co-founder

"I highly recommend *Daughter 4254* for anyone who enjoys a well crafted, engaging story. I would not be surprised to see this novel and its expected sequels eventually gain the popularity and acclaim of *Ender's Game*, *Maze Runner*, and similarly beloved works in the YA dystopian genre."

—Amazon Reviewer

# IMANI
## UNRAVELED

Leigh
Statham

OWL HOLLOW PRESS

Owl Hollow Press, LLC, Springville, UT 84663

Imani Unraveled

Library of Congress Cataloging-in-Publication Data
Imani Unraveled / L. Statham. — First edition.
Summary:

When her head is artificially filled with more information than she knows what to do with, Daughter4254 is faced with a choice she thought she'd left far behind when she'd walked from the doors of the compound.

ISBN 978-1-945654-25-1 (paperback)
ISBN 978-1-945654-26-8 (e-book)
LCCN 2018961103

For all the girls navigating this world on their own.
You're not alone.

T he wind scratches my cheeks with icy fingers. I round the corner of the building and look up, checking the rooftop for an autoeye. It still feels strange to be in a place where I'm not watched every second of every day. I keep thinking there has to be a guard somewhere or that a random person passing a window might notice me wandering alone in the side yard and call for an investigation. I don't think I'll ever lose those habits of apprehension from my life before prison and Secondary School.

I turn away from the quiet building and search the tree line ahead of me. *Did I really see Thomas?* I take a few more steps and stop at the dead, gray fruit tree outside my bedroom window. The glass is slightly mirrored, but not enough that I can't see inside. If he was here, he saw me.

I peer again across the clearing to the trees and rocks ahead. *Where did he go?*

My first instinct is to run, hoping to be faster than anyone who might be watching, but my failed history of running away keeps my steps slow and regular. Besides, the blanket of snow on the ground, untouched by anything larger than a rodent or bird, makes my footprints stand out like a big red arrow.

My head thumps with sudden pain as an image of a huge red arrow fills my vision, overtaking my tracks in the snow. *Neon* is the word my mind supplies. Before I can shake my head to clear it, the sign disappears and the pain eases off as well.

I take a deep breath. Hamen, who still feels like Professor789 to me, did a great job messing with my head. This is the third time since awaking in the Institute that I've had a strange flash of a memory that isn't mine. Each is accompanied by a word unfamiliar to me: *arpeggio* and *sunflower* and now *neon*.

Snow shifts on a nearby tree branch and cascades with soft plops onto the ground below. I tell myself to keep up the lie I started with the main door attendant.

*I need some fresh air. I'm going for a walk to clear my head.*

I felt certain they wouldn't let me just walk out of the Institute, but they did. The woman had been friendly and all smiles—another thing I wasn't used to. She gave me a thermal parka and some boots and warned me not to go too far from the Institute, that there were sometimes beasts lurking in the trees. A pang of guilt tugged at my gut as I thanked her.

I was not simply going for a walk. I was running for my life, and possibly for Thomas's life. For our life together.

I wrap my arms around myself in the puffy coat and rub my shoulders while I walk slowly across the clearing. My bare hands soon grow too cold for that, and I stuff them deep in the parka's pockets. The trees stand tall and brown against the white snow like an overgrown fence or a row of frozen soldiers. As I draw close to their rough brown bark and suck in the cold, clean air, I search for any sign of Thomas. Still nothing. I scan the ground at the edge of the trees where I thought I saw him from my room. Nothing, not even a footprint. My heart sinks.

If Thomas is dead, do I have any reason not to take Hamen's offer to stay and help him fight the Leaders subversively? At least I could help other people like me who are stuck in the system. But I still don't trust Hamen. He slipped too easily between the Leaders and the resistance and has lied to me about almost everything.

I take a few more steps into the dark shadows of the forest. The sunlight lingers behind me in the clearing. It is now or never. Walk forward or turn back. Run or stay.

I shove my hands into my pockets and step deeper into the woods, my feet scarring the fresh snow. I need to keep looking for something better than what I am leaving behind.

My first steps are slow. There is no sign that I'm being watched from the forest or the bright white building behind me. I make a silent promise to myself as my eyes well up with tears.

*I will not cry. I will not panic. I will walk away, go into the woods, disappear. There are people in the mountains, and I will find them. I will make a life for myself. I will do this, or I will die trying.*

I quicken my pace. My throat tightens further. Breathing through these thoughts and emotions is hard, and the crisp winter air makes it painful. My heart pounds twice as fast as my feet crunching through the snow. The trees fall in behind me, blocking the building from sight. Hope dangles on the edge of my thoughts, close to falling into a chasm of cynicism. There may not be any sign of Thomas, I may be lost to delusions, but I am walking. Choosing my own path and my own future, even for a moment.

Then I see it. Next to a large rock in the center of a beam of light cutting through the shadows of the forest—a fresh footprint.

I can't help myself—I sprint forward. I don't dare call out his name. It could be a trail from a guard or a Leader or forestry worker. Still, I look desperately from tree to tree and back to the trail of footsteps in front of me.

The steps come from deep in the woods and double back on themselves. I push through naked bushes and crisp evergreens dusted white with snow. My thick coat catches on the branches, making synthetic scratching sounds that set my nerves even more on edge. I want to take it off but my freezing face tells me that wouldn't be wise. The temperature is well below freezing.

The tracks keep going and I keep following while unwanted thoughts dance through my mind. *What if I saw someone but only thought it was Thomas? What if I didn't see anything, and these footprints are an illusion and I'm going mad?* After

Hamen described the procedure I underwent to store centuries' worth of data in my mind, I have no doubt that I could be delusional now, the part of brain that knows reality from daydreams permanently damaged.

An index of mental illnesses flash before my eyes, like the pages of a text book flipping in front of me while I read at top speed.

*Bipolar II disorder*

*Body dysmorphic disorder*

*Borderline intellectual functioning*

*Borderline personality disorder*

*Brief psychotic disorder*

*Bulimia nervosa*

I groan and shake my head, closing my eyes against a headache that pierces where the previous pain hit with the image of the red neon arrow. The pain dissipates again, as quickly as before, and I stand straight, not remembering hunching over. I must think about Thomas.

Thomas.

I take a step forward and a heavy weight hits my shoulders and back with such force I fall forward, hands only coming up in time to prevent my face from taking the brunt of the fall. I try to scream, but my face is shoved into the snow. The cold burns my cheeks as my nose is bent and scraped against a rock. Movement on my back precedes snarling hot breath in my ear.

I'm crushed deeper into the snow by the weight of a clawing mass. A flash of gratitude for the thick parka fills me as I hear it rip in several places, synthetic skin saving my own. I flail and fight to get out from under whatever has me pinned, but it's so heavy, I'm losing the battle. Finally, I swing back hard with an elbow and make my first solid contact. Whatever it is wobbles, off balance. I grab the chance to flip onto my back and start punching.

What I thought was a forest creature is a person, a man. But something is wrong with his eyes. They're too dark, too intense. Even in the dim forest light I can tell they are more animal than human. I shove and kick as hard as I can, trying to get him off of me. He slaps my cheek and pulls my hair. I punch and kick, screaming for help. The man grabs both of my arms, forcing them against the ground above my head, and shoves his face next to mine. I push my jaw against his, screaming in his ear, trying to keep his mouth away from my neck.

He snarls and roots at my shoulder. His breath is foul, like rotten flesh and sour milk. My arms are wedged up against his shoulders leaving only my head to defend myself from his mouth. I shove the top of my head against his cheek, trying to force it away. It is no use. Disgusting grunts and pants leave moist vapor on my skin until he rears back and crashes his forehead into mine. The blow knocks me senseless but in that same moment his weight is knocked off me.

When the stars and black dots leave my vision, I can see my attacker on the ground. Another man has him in a choke hold from behind, squeezing the air out of him until, all too quickly, he falls limp. I scoot backward until I bump against a large rock, then struggle to get to my feet so I can run, but I'm too slow.

The second man drops the first man and is on top of me, his hand over my mouth. My eyes sting with tears and I can't breathe from the shock. His face, covered in a mask like the one my father wore to work in the forest on the coldest winter days, hovers near mine as he secures me with strong arms, wedging me in a sitting position against the boulder and the snowy ground. Then one knee is on my legs while he straightens up to peer back down the trail over the rock that conceals us. His thick green coat is the confirmation I need to know he isn't a guard from Hamen's. They would be wearing a white coat like me. I don't know whether to be relieved or terrified.

Adrenaline still pumping through me, I strain to free my arms. It isn't too late to run. I can survive and find the mountain people.

But instead of attacking, he bends down and looks into my eyes before letting his hand slip off my mouth and his grip on my shoulder loosens.

Soft hazel eyes meet my panicked gaze, and I freeze. Even with the rest of his face covered, I know those eyes.

"Thomas!" The name comes out in a burst of white fog from my mouth.

He eases off of me and I pull up his mask to reveal his scruffy face, the same one I saw watching me through bars all those days and nights in prison. I want to hold him close like my mother used to hold me—he's so close anyway. But I hesitate. Thomas isn't like my mother. What would it feel like to hold him? It feels strange to consider it.

"Hush, lassie," he says. "They're bound to be right behind us."

At the sound of his voice, I can't hold back anymore. I throw my arms around him. All the moments of being without him and wishing I'd jumped with him melt between us as he returns my embrace and his breath warms my neck.

"What are you doing here?" I check my voice and whisper, "How did you find me? How are you alive? I can't..." I'm not sure what else to say, where to start.

"I'm a tough nut, you know?" He smiles and rubs my raw cheek with his wool glove. Mixed with my tears, the sweet gesture stings my skin, but I don't care.

"I can't believe you're alive." I pull him to me again and bury my face in his shoulder, my head pounding from the fight with the wild man.

His strong arms wrap around me, and I hear his voice echo in his chest. "Honestly, sweets, I can't believe you're not a walking veggie head. I want to hear all about your adventures as soon as we're out of these bloody woods. Come on."

Feeling his legs shift, I sit back and he helps me to my feet while scanning the trail behind us again.

"We're leaving a proper mess for them to follow so we've

got to scurry." He takes my hand and starts back over his footprints leading farther into the woods. "How did you get out here,
anyway? I didn't expect you to waltz into my arms like a crank-
ing birthday gift."

"I told them I was going for a walk. I know the leader—he
was trying to recruit me. He said I could do whatever I wanted,
but I overheard him saying that if I didn't comply they'd roast
me. Complete Mind Wipe." I am rambling now. Must focus.
"How did you find me? And who was that man? What was
wrong with him?"

As if on cue, there's motion behind us. Down the trail, the
beast man moans and sits up. Thomas pushes me behind him,
ready to knock the man out again if he approaches, but a *twang*
cuts through the air, and the man falls back to the snow, convulsing. Shock rifle fire.

"Come on, no time to chatter." Thomas pulls my arm, and
we run through the brush and trees, ignoring the footprints
Thomas made on his way to get me.

I can't help looking back. One man in a white suit is kneel-
ing to examine my attacker. Two others have spotted us and are
charging forward, long black shock rifles wagging back and
forth in front of their chests.

I know what those guns feel like. I know what happens
when they catch you. Shudders trip down my spine and I push
myself to keep up with Thomas, determined not to lose him this
time as we slalom tree trunks and trip through the snow.

Another *twang* rings through the air, and a branch a few feet to my left shatters.

"They are catching up," I say between breaths, feeling fear rise in my throat.

"No matter, we're here." He looks back at me and slows slightly. "You gonna trust me this time?"

"What?"

We emerge from the trees, and Thomas catches my arm so I don't fall down a steep, snowy embankment to a river two hundred yards below. The drop isn't as far as at the prison, but the water below is agitated and swift, frothing and white. I can see where Thomas has carefully picked his way up the hill farther upstream where large rocks jut out of the snowy hillside. Directly before us lies a slippery, snow-covered slide of unknown hazards. Behind, the soldiers' shouts sound on the other side of the tree line.

I look at Thomas and without hesitation, I jump.

## TWO

The snow is packed harder than I would have guessed. We slide much faster than we can control. I cling to Thomas's gloved hand with my own bare one and try not to scream. My forehead throbs centered around the knot swelling where the monster man headbutted me. The wind whips past my face, carrying pellets of ice kicked up from our feet trying to dig in and slow the descent. The river bank is coming up quickly. Too quickly.

"Thomas," I squeak out. I want to shut my eyes and brace for impact, but instead I watch in horror as jagged rocks lining the frozen river's edge grow larger, closer.

"Hang on, I gotcha." Thomas grips my hand tightly and bends his knees, digging his feet deeper into the icy snow bank.

*Twang.*

The guards must have reached the edge. But the sounds of their rifles are accompanied by the scraping of ice and metal, and Thomas begins to slow. Momentum carries me ahead of him, the motion centered on the connection of our hands. My arm fully extends and starts to strain, gravity fighting to pull my fingers from their grasp on his glove.

"I need both your hands," he yells.

I roll on my side and reach up, catching him around his free wrist with my flailing hand. I immediately feel the tug increase as he successfully slows my descent as well.

*Twang, twang.*

More shots.

"Hold on, we're gonna speed this up again." Thomas redoubles his grip on my right hand, then my left, before lifting his feet, and we shoot down the slope again.

This time I look down at the rocks and realize they are boulders and we are only a few moments away from smashing into them.

I look up the hill. The guards are standing at the top of the ridge, taking aim.

Pain in my temples is followed by snippets of shock rifle statistics flowing across my vision: diagrams, measurements, development. I shut my eyes and shake the information away, groaning. But now I know these rifles have limited range and accuracy. They aren't like the guns of the past, firing hundreds of feet with startling precision. We may be out of their reach on the river.

"Hang on!" Thomas yells as we slow more quickly this time, yanking on my outstretched arms. Then my feet slam into the boulders below, my legs buckling.

I open my eyes and scramble to my hands and knees. The

guards aren't following us, but that doesn't mean they will let us go. One puts his rifle down and speaks into a small black box. The other keeps us in his sights.

*Twang.*

The rock next to me explodes, little pebbles showering the ground around us.

Okay, so maybe I misjudged their range.

"Time to go, love." Thomas is on his feet and pulling me up too.

We slip around the huge rocks, coated in ice, to face the river in its roaring glory. I hope Thomas won't ask me to dive into the icy waters. I know we have to get out quickly, but I've never been in water deeper than a shower puddle. How will I survive the freezing current roaring in front of me?

As we round the corner between rocks and the last *twang* dies away behind us, I see a small boat tied to a scrawny tree, halfway lodged on a thin, sandy bank. Thomas takes off his gloves and hands them to me.

"Put these on," he says, and I do so quickly, savoring the warmth his hands left for mine. He stomps ahead and starts untying the line. Once it's free, he looks up at me.

I meet his gaze, understanding urgency that doesn't need to be spoken. I take in the river and the tiny wooden vessel. This is better than swimming, but I've never ridden in a boat either. We didn't live anywhere near water that used boats for any purpose, and recreational boating is not *of use*.

"Get in. No doubt they are calling up for ropes and the like so they can scale down and nab us."

"I've never been in a boat before. I-I don't know what to do," I stammer.

"Just get in and hold on. Don't dance around and we'll be fine." He smiles at me as he tugs at the ropes. The same smile that got me through all those days in prison, only now there are no bars separating us, no regulations, no guards—except the ones behind us on the hill.

I step gingerly into the shallow water and take hold of the brown wooden sides. As I lift my other leg up, the boat tips under my weight and I almost lose my balance. With one foot on the uneven bottom, I hurry to swing my other leg into the boat, shaking as I cling to the side. Shallow water pools around my boots as I wobble toward a small bench built in the back. I sit down and grasp both sides of the boat. They feel smooth even through Thomas's warm wool gloves, worn down by the hands of previous passengers holding on for their lives, I'm sure.

Thomas throws the ropes in after me and starts to push the boat into the current. As we slide away from the shore, the top of the hill rises into view beyond the large boulders sheltering us. The guards aren't visible, but I don't relax yet. My arms are tense and I flex my calves. Thomas was right. They are probably waiting for ropes or bigger guns or something worse before they come after us. Their whole existence, everything they cherish, is crammed in my brain, and they don't want that slipping out of their control.

Thomas gives one last push, then jumps expertly into the front of the boat. The slight rocking caused by his jump convinces me the boat is about to capsize and I squeeze the sides tighter, closing my eyes. My whole body tightens and I hold my breath as the boat lowers farther into the dark waters with Thomas's weight and then catches the current and speeds ahead. When I'm brave enough to open my eyes, Thomas is standing in front of me with a pole, pushing us away from an oncoming rock and catapulting us farther into the flow. I hold my breath as we shoot forward.

Not wanting to look at the raging river around us, I look down into the boat and notice Thomas's boots. Now that we aren't in the snow, I can see large metal spikes protruding from the soles. That must have been how he climbed up the hill and how he slowed our descent. An image of the spikes going through the brown wood in the bottom of the boat and water rising up around me makes me shiver, and I close my eyes again. He got down here without puncturing the boat, so we should be able to get out too.

I release the side of the boat to gently prod the spot where the wild man knocked his head against mine, and a dull throbbing meets my fingers. The backs of my eyelids light up accompanied by stabbing pain between my temples. I grab the sides of the boat again and brace myself for what comes next.

*RMS* Titanic *was a British passenger liner that sank in the North Atlantic Ocean on 15 April 1912 after colliding with an iceberg during her maiden voyage from Southampton, UK, to New York City, US. The sinking of* Titanic *caused the deaths of more than 1,500 people in one of the deadliest peacetime maritime disasters in modern history.*

"Stop, stop, stop!"

"Can't love. We're well on our way now. Look, they're giving up. Woo-hoo!"

Thomas doesn't realize I'm not talking to him.

This pain, these information flashes, are the byproducts of Hamen messing with my head. After Thomas escaped the prison and I was taken to the Mind Wipe, Hamen filled me with all the lost information of our ancestors—everything our current Leaders had decided wasn't *of use*, including most history, art, and music. What he hadn't told me was that random bits would pop up without warning in flashes and bursts of pain. I can't decide if I'm glad to have it or if I wish it was back in Hamen's machine.

As soon as the episode has passed—in a moment that feel like several minutes—I look up. In the distance, the guards have both dropped their weapons and are watching us. We are moving too fast for them to catch. The river bends to the left, taking us with it. An outcropping of trees on the bank passes between us and they are gone. I wonder what Hamen will say when he finds out I ran away. I picture his face growing dark and morphing into the man I knew best, the man who enjoyed tormenting students in Secondary School. The man who wouldn't hesitate to erase my personality and memories if given the chance.

How could he have ever been, as he claims, my mother's friend?

The river is still swift but is deep and smooth now. I grow used to the gentle rocking, and seeing Thomas confident at the helm helps me relax. At each section of rapids, Thomas guides us through expertly. He looks back at me now and then, a broad smile splitting his handsome face. As I think about how much I missed him—his voice, his smile, the mischief in his eyes—I realize that I don't know this wild mountain boy much better than I know Hamen. Yet I am willing to trust him, to follow him this time. Though he could be taking me to a life much worse than Hamen offered, I doubt it with my whole heart. Any life that includes Thomas is better than one without him.

I wish I'd never doubted him the first time.

# THREE

After what has to be at least an hour on the boat, my stomach twists and my eyes feel heavy, despite the cold. Or maybe because of it. I wish that I would have gone to eat with Hamen immediately after I woke up. But I shake away those thoughts, reminding myself that I would have missed seeing Thomas outside my window.

Thomas. Now that I've had a chance to examine him more closely, I notice his dark hair has been trimmed. His beard, so rough and patchy from neglect in prison, has been shaved and is growing back. Dark stubble dusts his jaw and chin. He sits straight and tall at the front of the boat, guiding it with a long stick. As if feeling my gaze, he turns to smile, revealing bright white teeth, crooked enough to make it obvious he's not from the city. He looks so happy, but his eyes have dark circles etched under them. I wonder if he has found anything to eat or a warm place to sleep during the days I was in the Institute having my brain rewired.

The jagged dark gray rocks and needle-laden evergreen trees on the shoreline are blanketed with soft white snow. Focusing on them helps to keep my attention as I try not to think about the boat tipping over or the frigid temperature of the water. As I relax, I realize the names of the trees we pass, their life cycles, their uses, are slipping painlessly through my mind. I let the information flow through my mind instead of fighting it. When I try to focus on any particular detail, the flow pauses but a headache threatens to blossom, and I let the information flow through me like the river rushing by on either side. I wonder how many people Hamen pumped full of this lost information. Where are they now?

"Oy, love!" Thomas calls out over the sound of the river. "Check that knapsack there, would ya?"

I look at the floor of the boat where he is pointing to a dirty brown bag gathered at the top by two crude laces. The bottom third of it appears darker than the rest, soaked by a bucket's worth of water sloshing in the bottom of the boat.

I pull the bag between my feet, not wanting the wet bottom on my pants, and stick my hands in the hole, pulling the laces loose, then open. My mouth begins to water. Inside are bread, apples, and dried meat, all protected from the water by a wax lining.

"Where did you get this?" I say. "Where have you been staying the last few days?"

"I've got friends under every rock." He winks at me. "Help yourself."

I reach in and pull out the apple first. I can't remember the last time I ate one. The food rationing was so severe in the weeks before I left Secondary School that many of my friends were starving. I shared my meals—reward for doing well in my classes—and rarely ate more than bread and canned fish most days. Prison food was actually a step above that, offering an occasional bowl of mush or unidentifiable overcooked vegetable.

Now I hold a bright yellow apple covered in tiny brown spots like the freckles on the face of a child. I turn it over in my hands, appreciating it, then take a huge bite. The fruit is cold and stings my teeth, but the juice is sweet and dribbles over my lips and down my chin. I wipe my mouth with the back of my hand. I'm embarrassed to find Thomas watching me, but his expression is pure joy.

"It's good, yah?" he says just as I say, "It's so good." We both laugh and end up talking over each other again.

"Have you ever had—" Thomas starts.

"Thank you so much," I interrupt him.

"Ladies first," he says and holds out a hand indicating I should speak. We don't have to lower our voices for fear of being overheard by guards. The freedom is intoxicating and terrifying.

"I have had one before, but it wasn't this good," I say through bites of apple, answering his unfinished question. I chew and swallow, then ask, "Do you want one?"

He shakes his head, his smile so bright, so rewarding. He's happy because I am happy, and that is enough for both of us.

"Where are we going?" I ask.

Images of tall, thick men with dark red beards and stern faces flash through my mind. They have swords and axes and are obviously warriors. I push them away and try to focus on Thomas's answer.

"My people. The mountain folk. Only they don't exactly live on the mountains anymore."

"Oh?"

"Aye. After the batty old lady ratted on us, they moved back into the mountains. Under them, I suppose you could say."

"How do you live under the mountains?"

"Where do you think they get all those fancy metals for all the fancy gadgets your folk are so fond of?"

"I don't know." That is the truth. I haven't ever thought about where the materials came from to supply us with trucks and pods or even circuitry for doors and autoeyes.

"The mountains, lass, and we're the trolls that dig it out for you."

"Then you were in contact with the Leaders before they raided your village? I thought you hid from them." My daydreams of running off to join the mountain people always involved a community far from the influence of the Leaders and their society, not part of it.

"We hide our way of life. They think we are a part of your system, but we're not. We never were."

"Don't call it *my* system." I turn away from him and take

another big bite of the apple.

He's quick to apologize. "Sorry, I didn't mean it that way."

But something else he said has already distracted me. "Why did the Leaders raid your village in the first place? Was it only because of illegal activity?" I've never heard of Leaders letting a community get away with any kind of subversion without severe retribution, but clearly the mountain people have continued their way of life.

"That and we were starting to push back on their demands, asking for more in return for the metal we sent to them. There's been talk of splitting off from the Leaders for a while now. Everyone is pretty fed up, but there are two different groups of thought among my people."

I nod at him to continue, soaking up the information about the people I've longed to join my whole life.

"Some want to split off and fight the Leaders, try to gain back some of our land and set up our own government. Others want to keep things low and slow. They want to be free of the Leaders, but no war."

"No one wants to stay with the current government?"

"Would you?" he asks, smiling at me.

"Good point," I say. "Where do you fall?"

"I'm a lover, not a fighter," he says, then points ahead. "We're nearly there. Just around the bend and then we hike up the mountain a bit."

He looks back to the river and the sound of the water fills

the silence between us. I may have a lot of old-world history crammed in my head, but the information Thomas revealed about his people is brand new, and I'm struggling to fit it in with my experience of the Leaders and their world. The job of navigating the river keeps Thomas busy for the moment, but as he works the pole to steer the boat around the bend and toward a sandy shore, my heart starts to race, anxiety kicking in again.

When we land on dry ground, it will just be me and Thomas. Nothing between us. I have never been alone with a boy before. There were always autoeyes watching or a Leader or parent around the corner, bars separating us in prison. Even now, there is a boat on the verge of capsizing and the need to escape. And this is Thomas. His dark hair and strong face are so familiar to me. His hand on the pole, guiding the boat like he guided me through each miserable day when we were locked up. His ready smile even when the situation is bleak. His quick laugh and the way he openly shows affection. He's free from the laws I grew up with, free from all of my hesitations and fears. I feel my breathing quicken and my palms grow hot in the cold winter air when I think about being free like that, forever, with him.

With a soft grinding of wood on sand, our boat catches on the river's edge. Thomas cries, "Here we are!" and jumps into the shallow water, circling around to the back of the boat to push it farther onto land.

I throw what's left of the gnawed apple core into the water

and stand, wobbling, with the crude knapsack clutched to my chest with one hand and the side of the boat with the other as I work my way to the front.

*The front of a boat is the bow.*
*The back of a boat is the stern.*
*When a person is facing the bow, left side is port and the*
right side is starboard.

The information, unbidden, is accompanied by a stabbing pain behind my right eye.

"Got it," I whisper through the pain and try to focus on climbing out the bow without re-soaking my already wet shoes and feet.

"What's that?" Thomas wades around to the side and offers me his hand.

The pain from the memory fades, leaving me slightly dazed. I look at his hand, trying to understand why it's there. It's rough, darker than mine, nails chewed to their beds and crisscrossed with lines that seem drawn on with a writing tool instead of creased by nature. Do I want to touch that hand? I clutch the bag closer to my chest.

"What is it?" His voice sounds as if it is coming through a fog. "Imani?"

Startled by my name, I remember I'm with Thomas; this is Thomas's hand, Thomas who helped me stay sane in prison and escape the revolutionaries. Did my hesitation hurt his feelings? He definitely isn't wearing his usual happy-go-lucky smile.

I take his hand in mine. Even through the glove I can feel that his fingers are like chunks of ice. I feel selfish and cruel all at once. Of course, he is freezing. He is standing in a frozen river, patiently waiting while I decide if I trust him or not.

He came back for me. Even after I abandoned him on the cliffside in the prison yard, watching him fall and then be shot. How could I not go with this boy now? How could I not trust him? All of that aside, I want to go, to find something new.

I use his arm to step carefully out of the boat and onto the beach, avoiding the icy waters. Once we are both on dry land, I drop the bag and tackle him in an embrace. Hopefully it'll both warm him up and act as an apology for not taking his hand sooner.

"Whoa there, darling." He laughs and hugs me back.

I bury my face in his chest and close my eyes, letting the warmth of our connection spread through my body. When Thomas speaks, the words rumble through his chest.

"This feels mighty nice and all, and I'd love to warm up together any other day, but we've got a ways to go and I'm not sure those fellas are done following us."

I step back, my face burning red, and look around for guards or a trail or something other than Thomas. "I'm sorry."

"Don't be. Give me a hand with the boat, will ya?"

He drags the boat past the sand and into the twigs and grass bordering the snowline. I take a few quick steps forward and grab the rope above him. He motions for me to take a hold of one side as he takes the other. The boat is surprisingly light. We easily lift it high enough to clear the snow, and I follow him into the woods.

"Right here's good." He motions to a giant fir tree with large branches reaching the ground in all directions, ends buried in snow "Just hold it steady a second."

He braces the boat on his knee and tugs a branch's end out of its snowy confines. Once he lifts it up, I can see a dry area under the tree large enough for three boats like the one we are carrying. In fact, there is another boat tucked in the space, like a sleeping bear waiting for spring, along with a large wooden chest.

We stow our boat next to its brother, then Thomas opens the trunk and digs around while I admire our secret hiding place.

We didn't have trees this large in the community I grew up in. I try to guess its age by the circumference of its trunk, nearly twice that of the trees I am used to. How does such a tree exist when all the flora and fauna were wiped out a few decades earlier? Maybe it is a different hybrid. I run my fingers down rough bark of the trunk.

"How old do you think this tree is?" I ask, wondering if Thomas might know having grown up on the mountain.

"Older than us, that's for sure. These aren't the quick producing trees the Leaders put out for their mills. These are the

Douglas firs that survived the devastation or sowed themselves and grew up from the ashes of the wars."

"They seeded themselves?"

"Yup."

"But I thought nothing could grow after the wars. I thought the land was wasted and barren after the Neuroadvanced came out of their bunkers."

"Do you believe everything those fancy pantsers tell you down there?" He motions back up the river in the direction we came from.

I close my mouth and think about what he's said. He is right. There are plenty of things the Leaders lied about. I wonder for a moment how much of what is in my head might be a lie as well. How will I be able to tell what is real and true?

"Here it is." He pulls something out of the chest. "Dry clothes and some better boots for ya, lassie." He hands me a pair of thick green woolen pants and brown boots, then goes back to digging around in the chest. "There are socks inside the boots as well."

Dry clothes sound very nice, but I hesitate. "Thank you, Thomas, that's wonderful, but… where am I supposed to change?"

"No better place than right here." He turns around holding his own pair of dry pants and boots in his hands, a wicked grin creasing his cheeks.

For a split second I regret the hug I'd thrown so carelessly at him earlier. Maybe I'd given him the wrong idea. Or the right idea at the wrong time? Then again, maybe it is normal for boys and girls to see each other change clothes where he comes from. I grew up under the constant watch of the autoeye, but that's not the same thing as a live human boy standing in front of me while I strip to my underwear beneath a tree in the middle of nowhere and with no supervision.

My shock must be clear because he laughs.

"I'm fooling, lassie! I'll be out there clearing up some of our tracks. You get yourself dry and ready and holler at me when it's safe for me to come back in. Alrighty?"

I breathe a sigh of relief and feel my cheeks burn hot again. Unbidden, the memory of his kiss on the cliff just before he jumped over the edge shoots from my head to my feet, and I long to revisit that kind of closeness. Somehow my cheeks burn even hotter and a heat matching it rises in my abdomen.

I step aside and look down as he walks straight at me on his way to leave our shelter. But he pauses in front of me and puts his cold hand on my hot cheek.

"It's a good day, Imani." As if he had read my mine, his eyes twinkle as his lips press into mine, warm and full.

As soon as it happens it's over, and he is ducking under the branch, humming a tune as he makes his way back to the shore.

# FOUR

We leave our wet clothes strewn out on the dry inner branches of the Douglas fir, and Thomas leads me to a small creek that somehow resisted winter's ice and has carved a path through the snow. Steam rises from its bubbling rivulets. I lean over and touch it with my bare hands; it's as warm as bathwater.

"Those boots are waterproof. We'll start out on the bank, but we'll be in the creek soon enough. If we pick our way carefully up the rocks, they won't know where we're going."

"Why is the water so warm?" I think of the factories in the pre-war days using water to cool their oil-soaked machinery then dumping it, hot and contaminated, back into the earth.

"Geothermal heat. The earth bubbles it up all hot and smelly then spits it out and down the mountain, but not before we have our way with it."

"What do you mean?" I say.

"You'll see when we get to where we're going. Hot water's got lots of hidden power. Very nice in a bath too. Fancy a bath?" He raises his eyebrows at me, and my stomach grows hot again.

Then I recall the large, modern bathroom I'd left at the Institute. I wonder how long it will be before they drain the unused water I left behind.

Thomas walks behind me with a large fir branch swiping back and forth over our tracks in the snow. He is leaving a bigger trail then we originally carved with our boots, but he assures me that the soft white flakes starting to fall will fill in our trail before we are half a mile away. New snow will fall that night, and no one will know we were ever there.

After about a mile, the bank of the creek gets rockier. Thomas ditches the branch and we begin to hike up the creek's center, Thomas in the lead. We hike quietly, taking our time. The creek bed is wide, and the clear water falls from one shallow pool to another, ice forming at the edges around the tiny pebbles. I am desperately out of shape after sitting in prison for months. My breath comes hard and heavy, billowing giant white clouds in front of my face. The muscles in my legs already strain from the effort of our uphill climb. The trees and rocks are all blanketed in deep snow, lending a hush to the landscape that muffles our voices and the sounds of passing creatures.

I hear a few birds calling, but I can't get a close enough look to tell what their type. I wonder if they would be allowed in the valley below or if they are like my little yellow songbirds the Leaders shot without thinking twice.

*To protect the crops and seed harvests. If we let one live they will multiply and devastate our efforts.*

The cold air and exertion clear my mind of inserted memories, and I enjoy the mental reprieve and silence, focusing instead on each step so I don't turn an ankle. The wind picks up after a few moments and more large white flakes of snow float down around us. A few land on Thomas's dark hair, creating a beautiful contrast. I can't help but think of white and yellow feathers as I watch the flakes flit back and forth, weaving a blanket of camouflage.

I hope Thomas is right and this will be enough to cover our tracks.

"Thomas?" I ask after a few minutes of hiking in the creek. "Who was the man who attacked me in the woods? What was wrong with him?"

"I'm not sure, but I'll wager he's one of Hamen's test subjects. Our spies reported that they had a few get loose from the labs. Never know what you'll get when you mess with a person's brain."

I shudder as I remember being connected to Hamen's equipment.

"Speaking of brains, how's yours?" Thomas asks. He sounds nonchalant, but he glances back at me, his eyes serious.

I don't know what to say. I don't want to think about it, so I change the subject.

"Were you a miner too?"

Thomas only pauses a moment. "Miner in training. We still follow the job assignment regulations your folk… I mean, the

Leaders set up down below. My whole family is a rash of miners and bakers. My mother is the best cook you'll ever have the pleasure to eat with."

"You cook your own food?"

"Aye, don't you?"

"No. I mean, we heated stuff up, but it was delivered weekly in assigned proportions."

"Huh." He pauses. "Like prison then, eh?"

"I suppose so." Then I remember something else I wanted to ask him. "Where did you get your food and the boat from?"

"Our folk have been watching the prison ever since they took half of us away, hoping we were sittin' in there. After I made it down the hill, I followed the river to an old outpost I knew of and was lucky enough to run into a pack of them what were getting ready to bust us out."

"You're joking?"

"Naw, only I told them there weren't many of us left, just the ranting old lady and a couple of others that were getting the wipe soon. They decided to call it quits and head back home."

"Why didn't you go with them?" I ask.

"I couldn't leave you up there, could I?"

"But how did you know I wasn't a vegetable like the rest of them? You knew I'd get the wipe as soon as they caught me."

"I figured there was a chance they might be holding you for something else. I heard some rumors about you, ya know," he says, and smiles.

"From who?"

"The guards, mostly. Other prisoners. There were stories of a revolution going on, started by a wee lass in a secondary school somewhere. But the folks who came to bust us out confirmed my guesses and filled in lots more details."

I almost trip. "A revolution?"

"Aye." Thomas grins. "You were the only lass I'd seen at the prison in months. Figured it was you they were all jabbering on about."

I consider his words as we trudge up the creek. It could be nothing. It could be everything.

"What kind of revolution?" I almost don't want to know. Considering what the Leaders were capable of when we were merely fooling around with schoolwork, I don't want to think about what they would do to put down an actual mutiny.

"I heard there was fighting in a couple of provinces. Folks barricaded themselves in your secondary school and a couple of government buildings. One of the train lines was hijacked and a load of food and weaponry went missing."

I stop.

Thomas takes a few steps then stops and looks back at me, his grin fading. "What's the matter? I thought you'd be bouncing in your boots at the news of the success."

Is that what this is? I set out to show my fellow students that there was more to life than what the Leaders were giving us, and I end up starting a war. My muscles feel heavy and tight. I don't know whether to cry or laugh hysterically.

Thomas must sense my imminent breakdown. He takes a step toward me, hand out. "Imani, it's okay. It's not your fault, not really."

That tips the bucket.

"Not my fault? People are fighting, stealing weapons and food, and *dying*, Thomas. Because of something I did."

Thomas shakes his head slowly, expression serious. "It's been a long, long time coming. You just gave them all a shove in the back end."

"But that's not what I meant to do. I didn't mean for it to be a… a revolution." I speak in a whisper. Hot tears burn my cold cheeks as I try not to think about what people will do with those weapons, who would die, what would come next.

"Over there!" The harsh voice cuts through the blanketed landscape, distant but clear.

"Crappo," Thomas mutters then drops to a crouching position and pulls me down hard with him. "That's not my folk. They're as quiet as the day is long around here. We've gotta get going. Tip-toe like. Plenty of time to talk about what you did and didn't do on purpose later."

The knowledge of enemies nearby distracts me from Thomas's news, and I wipe my tears. Now is the time to focus on survival and escape.

We stay low for a minute, waiting to see if we've been discovered. The voice came from my right, but I can't see anyone and don't hear anything else for a few moments. Thomas gives my hand a quick squeeze as we slowly stand, then he hops up the creek. I follow close behind, exposed in the opening between trees the water had carved.

"Back here!" Another voice calls out, farther behind us and still to the right.

Thomas picks up his pace and I follow. He points ahead, and I hope that means we're almost to our destination.

A few more random calls bounce behind us, but they don't seem to be getting closer. Still, my heart beats and lurches in my chest, and I'm close to vomiting the cherished apple I ate too quickly.

"Here we go," Thomas murmurs as he ushers me to the left where a narrow dirt path is shielded by branches and shrubs. Occasional animal tracks make it a clear trail to the water. I've never seen tracks like these before, and I wonder what other strange creatures are hiding in the mountains. A list of animals rolls behind my eyes, accompanied by photographs of each in the wild and sketches of their tracks.

*Bear*

*Deer*

*Moose*

*Goat*

*Raccoon*

The small spilt hoof tracks are from an animal called a deer, dainty and light, covered in soft tan hair with patches of white, its large brown eyes reminiscent of a child's, confused and cautious.

"Fast now, lassie. We're almost to the opening." Thomas's voice brings me back to the moment.

We dart up the small path, winding around trees and bushes until we come to a small cliff face, about thirty feet high.

"Tracks over here!" The shout is closer behind us this time. They are catching up.

"Hold tight." Thomas ducks behind an outcropping of bushes at the foot of the cliff and I follow. For a few steps we walk between branches and stone wall until I see a small opening in the solid rock right against the snowy earth. It looks the right size for a badger, not a human.

"Password or die."

The voice from nowhere startles me.

"Onward ho," Thomas says with conviction.

"State your name and purpose."

"For crap's sake, Jake, it's me, Thomas. I'm back from the river and the bad guys're following me. Let us in!"

"What the... Thomas?" The head of a young boy peeks out of the hole and gazes at us with large eyes. "Who's the girl?"

"This is Imani. Would you just get out of the way? There's Leaders behind us. We're losing time."

"You let them follow you here?"

"I didn't *let* them. I did my best to hide our tracks. But I'm fresh outta guns and grenades now so I can't stop them. Let us in and go tell the guard."

"Sure," the boy says, "but I still want to know where you got the girl. She looks like a Leader to me." His eyes narrow.

"Jake!" Thomas's voice is dangerously loud.

The head disappears and Thomas motions for me to crawl in the hole. I hit my knees and do as he orders. Compared to the brightness of sun and snow outside, the tunnel is pitch black and a tight fit. I crawl forward until I feel the dark space open up around me and I hear voices. I curl up in a ball trying to make myself as small as possible, waiting for my vision to adjust.

Thomas is right behind me. He touches my shoulder. "It's okay, you can stand up."

I blink my eyes several times, willing them to adjust more quickly. The light from the opening spills into the cave for several feet. Objects start to take shape: a desk, a small lantern lighting up the opposite wall. As the room comes into focus, I realize that the space is much bigger than I'd anticipated. In fact, it is huge.

The ceiling is at least fifteen feet above my head, the room a good ten feet across. Beyond the desk is an opening in the room's wall—another tunnel, I presume. Guns line the wall behind it, and paper readers are stacked neatly by the little lamp. I guess there is plenty of time to sit and read while watching the tiny entrance for intruders.

The boy who questioned us appears in the mouth of the tunnel with two large men behind him. I wonder how they ever

got through the hole behind me. Maybe they'd been born underground and grew too big to get out.

"Welcome home, Thomas," one of the men says. "What's
the status?" He has a thick accent just like Thomas's, but his
voice is much deeper, much more serious. The accent doesn't
sound like it fits.

"Left the river crew two days ago. Collected Imani here and
used a raft to return. Stowed the raft, covered snow tracks and
used the creek bed to hike up, but they followed us. I'm not sure
how—I followed all regulations, honest."

Thomas sounds so serious. Does anyone smile here? This
new, dark place is making me uneasy, and a thread of fear works
its way into my heart.

"Probably used heat registers. No worries, we'll take them
down," the other man says. Each grabs a shock rifle and miracu-
lously slithers out the small opening as if covered in grease.

"What does he mean, take them down?" I sound like a
child, but I don't want any more blood on my hands. Another
thought strikes me. "And didn't the Leaders build these mines?
Don't they already know how to get in and out of here?"

Thomas takes my hand, and suddenly the dark room feels
less scary. "Aye, lassie, the Leaders and Hamen's men know the
locations of the topside entrances to the mines. They're always
watching 'em, hoping to track our movements after we went underground after the raids. But there are dozens of other exits that
only a few of us know about. Some folks captured during the

raids gave up the locations of some, and ever since, both the Leaders and Hamen have been trying to stop up the others. It would be all over if they pinned us down in here, so we have to keep as much hidden as possible."

The wind picks up outside and howls at the cave entrance, blowing bits of snow onto the dark earthy ground. Two *cracks* in rapid succession sound loudly outside our hiding place. Our trackers had gotten very close, but I hate that people are going to be hurt—have been hurt, or worse, died—and it is my fault. I squeeze his hand tightly, trying to release the pressure building in my chest.

"Come on," he says, leading me deeper into the mountain. "Let's get out of here."

"Thomas!" The shrill squeal rings through the massive underground room full of tables and chairs. A chorus of high-pitched voices join in, calling his name. A stampede of boys in loose brown pants and multicolored shirts and girls in long, colorful skirts and cropped hair jump up from the tables they'd been seated at and run toward us.

The space is finished like a building the Leaders might have made. The high ceilings are smooth and covered in white tile. Circular openings in the ceiling refract sunlight through long tubes above and fill the space with natural light. Supplemental lights hang on chains and add to the already bright room, making it feel cheery and welcoming, unlike the passages we just left. The walls are also covered in white tile, some painted with brightly colored images of flowers, strange animals, and swirling line designs. On the wall nearest us, I can make out tiles bearing names and dates. Seeing the hand-drawn pictures—illegal on the surface—is a forceful reminder that I am finally away from the Leaders.

"Hullo," Thomas calls. He gives my hand a tight squeeze before the crowd descends. Most of the girls are close to my age. Two are very small and cling to Thomas's legs like little animals. Their clothes are made from a variety of fabrics sewn together to make the fitted tops and full skirts. They look like a field of wildflowers, every color of the rainbow dancing in and out of their legs. A few men and women stand up and join the throng, reaching to pat Thomas's shoulders in welcome.

He begins to embrace the gathering group one by one. I step back, pressing up against the wall, out of the group of swishing skirts and trousers, to assess the situation.

Everyone is smiling and embracing. I've never seen anything like it. Back home, when my mother held me, we had to do it in the bathroom, away from the autoeye. The one time we were caught, they rationed our food and Mother had to take an extra shift at the textile mill. She still slipped in a hug or a kiss here and there, but I never saw affection between other people. It is unheard of to have a whole group of people laughing, smiling, and holding one another—in public, no less.

But in spite the strangeness of it all, it feels right. My gut swells with warmth telling me this is how it's supposed to be. For a few moments, I let myself bask in the relief of having arrived, of feeling the care the group has for one another. I close my eyes and take a deep breath, as though I might be able to smell happiness.

When I open my eyes, there is a small girl reaching for

Thomas, a lovely smile on her face. She reminds me of my dormmate 345 in Secondary School. But while 345 died from starvation, this girl's cheeks are plump and full, and her hair is sleek and short, not pulled back tight and braided into a rope down her back. Her clothes are mostly red, not the gray we were forced to wear up above. They make her skin glow a healthy pink. She is smiling. 345 didn't smile often. We didn't have any reason to smile.

I can't help but imagine the Leaders finding this haven, these rooms ringing with laughter and joy, and cutting it all down. They would tame this place of colorful skirts and painted tiles and embraces, return it to oppressive grayness.

Or perhaps I will be the one to ruin Thomas's home. Like I ruined my school with sabotage.

I feel a familiar tightness closing off my chest again, panic making its way into my lungs and heart. How many people back in the woods, at the school, in my home town, are dead because of my selfishness in wanting to get here? All my life I wanted to live somewhere that I could be free to be myself, to express myself, to sing and dance and have more than a number. But now that I am in the middle of it, I'm not sure if I can handle it.

The colored skirts and the white tiles and the bright lights swirl together, the laughter and the cries of joy mixing into a roar of noise.

There is just so much to take in. I press against the back wall, feeling trapped. My palms spread out on the cool tile, trying to hold the walls back from closing in.

It's too much. Too much.

Everything around me is swallowed in black and I feel my-self falling.

 **SIX**

I wake in a nest of soft cotton quilts atop a bed of rough-hewn logs. The room is much smaller than the white-tiled cafeteria I last remember being in. I am still in the clothes I traveled in, but my coat is sitting on a chair next to my cot and a thick quilt lies draped over me in its place. My boots are by the closed wooden door that stands at the opposite end of the room from my bed. A candle sits on a small table at the end of my bed, the soft glow bobbing and dancing around the dark walls. The room is circular with stone hewn walls and a low ceiling.

The memory of the bright faces clamoring around Thomas, all of them seeking his attention, comes back to me. Their dresses looked like something out of an ancient reader in the archives at school—long skirts and tight tops in every color of the rainbow. More color than I had ever seen, colors I didn't even know existed, worn as casually as I used to wear socks on a cold morning. Some even had adornments in their short hair—bright-colored ribbons made to look like flowers or birds. They were beautiful.

Then there was me. The last time I saw my reflection was in

my room at the Institute after Hamen's surgery. My long dark hair hung like a wall against my sallow skin. Circles under each brown eye looked more like bruises than the result of sleepless nights and poor nutrition. My loose white jumper was only exciting because it was different than the gray clothes I had worn the rest of my life. I've never worn a rainbow like these girls, and I don't feel quite worthy of starting now. What must they have thought of me when I collapsed in the middle of their congratulating Thomas on escaping the clutches of the evil flatlanders? Embarrassment blazes on my cheeks, and I close my eyes, trying to think of other things. I wonder how long I slept. I wonder where Thomas is now.

I stretch and sit up, only to gasp as pain shoots through my head. My probing fingers find a large knot above my right temple. I must have hit it when I passed out. I lie back down and take a deep breath. Two blows to the head in one day can't be good. I decide to go back to sleep. Maybe if I wait long enough they won't remember me as the strange new girl who passed out in front of everyone and knocked herself in the head.

The door opens just as I am drifting off again. At first, I pretend like I am still unconscious, but then curiosity gets the better of me when I hear shuffling feet and deep sighs. I stretch and open my eyes slowly to meet the gaze of my visitor.

The brownish-green eyes belong to the largest woman I have ever seen. The Leaders strictly monitored our diet—and by extension our weight—in the flat lands. No one ever had enough food to gain extra weight. This woman has a roll of flesh between her chin and neck, and the seams of her plain brown dress strain to contain arms larger than a man's. She is clearly strong, formidably so—it wouldn't be easy to push her around. Her face is ruddy and glistens with sweat, and her skin is sprinkled with freckles and moles. She examines me closely from top to bottom. Her hair is pulled back in a knot at the back of her head, and even though her size and sweatiness are off putting, her face breaks into a kind smile when our eyes meet, and she has the distinct smell of cinnamon and sugar—two things I love and haven't eaten in years.

I blink a few times and take a deep breath.

"You going to make it, lass?" Her voice is deep and pleasant, thick with accent. Thomas wasn't lying when he told me everyone talked like him *back home.*

"I think so," I croak.

"Tommy says you've had a rough few days." She stares in a disconcerting way, like she's evaluating my worth on the planet.

*Tommy?*

"I suppose I have," I say.

"You needn't worry about none of that here. You can rest and sleep and eat and get to feeling better. We'll take care of you."

"Thank you." I don't want to sound rude, but I have to know. "Who are you?"

"I'm Tommy's mother then, aren't I? It's my job to look after all the things he drags home." She laughs heartily at her own joke. I want to crawl under the covers and die. Am I just another thing he dragged home?

"Now then, don't be looking so sad and forlorn. I was only trying to coax a smile out of you. Life is good here in the mines. Sure, I miss my little house in the sunshine, but I'm grateful to have my boy back and a roof over my head, even if it is made of thousands of pounds of solid stone."

I think of my own thin, sometimes frail mother. I wondered if she and this hulking woman would have been able to sit and laugh together about the state of the world.

"What should I call you?"

"My name's spelled M-a-i-r-e, but it's pronounced Mara. I find you city folk have trouble getting your tongues around it."

"That's…" I try to think of a compliment, but everything is so new. I'm not used to people having proper names. I feel I have to explain this to her so she understands my confused reaction. "They all had numbers where I come from. Mine was 4254. That's what I've been called my whole life. I'm only just getting used to being called Imani—my mother's name. The name Thomas gave me."

Maire nods and pats my leg through the quilt. "It's okay. I know you're going through a lot of changes right now. Are you hungry? I made you up some breakfast."

"Breakfast?"

"Yep. You slept through the night. Thought for sure you

were either dead or straight out of a fairy tale."

"What's a fairy tale?"

As soon as the words are out of my mouth, my head explodes in pain and a mass of images and words.

*Once upon a time...*
*In a land far, far away...*
*It was a dark and stormy night...*

Maire is talking but I can't hear her. I grab my temples and moan, then wince as I bump the knot on my head and a new agony sets in. At least the flow of information stopped.

"Good heavens. What's ailing you now?" She steps closer and pulls my hands away to examine the large lump. "That's a nasty whack you got there. I think you're going to live though." She pulls a jar out of a pocket in the folds of her skirt and tucks a lock of my hair behind my ear before she smears the medicine on my bump. She doesn't seem to notice how her careful, casual touch makes me freeze.

"One thing's for certain, lass—you need a bath. I'm going to go draw up some hot water. We'll have time to talk of fairy tales after you've bathed. See if you can pull yourself together enough to eat that food." She puts the lid back on the bottle while she talks and pockets it as she heads out the door.

The reminder of food brings me to attention. I watch her close the door then scan for the breakfast she mentioned. Next to the candle on the small table is a tray with a mug and a plate covered in eggs, meat, and a bun dusted in cinnamon and sugar, still steaming from the ovens. My mouth waters—real food!

I sit up, ignoring the stabbing in my temple, and reach for the tray, pulling it to me like a long-lost friend. I try to take it slow, but everything tastes so good. I make it halfway through the plate before I have to set it back down on the table and rest; my stomach feels like it is going to burst. We'd have about that much food for meals during good weeks at home. At school we never got that much and never that quality, and in prison there was plenty, but it was barely edible.

I look for a place to stash the leftovers for when I am hungry again. Then I realize how foolish that is—this isn't prison or Secondary School or home. This is a new place that apparently has plenty of food. And beautiful colors everywhere. And public hugging.

I begin to feel overwhelmed again, so I focus on the quilt on my bed. I'm studying it, admiring its intricate triangle patterns and shades of yellow, when the door opens again.

Maire steps in holding a robe and towels that she sets at the foot of my bed. "How'd you like it?" She smiles and puts both hands on her hips as if she dares me to say it was anything other than amazing.

"It was amazing!"

"Good. You could use some meat on those little bones. Now, come with me. We're going to get you scrubbed up and put you to work. Nothing like hard work to get the past washed away. Water for the dirt, work for the hurt."

Picking up the towel and robe she's brought, I step gingerly to the floor, slip on my boots, and follow her out of my little circle room. The passageway is lined with similar wooden doors and lit by small round glowing circles in the ceiling. Some doors are open, some shut. Inside I see more little cots and sparse furnishings.

Maire notices my curiosity. "These used to be the storage rooms when this was strictly a mine. We had proper homes up above. Still keep a few guard houses and gardens up there, but mostly we all moved inside after the raids started. That's when they took my Tommy. Since our family is one of the biggest, we moved into this corridor of the mine so's the children could have their own rooms."

"How big is your family?"

"I have nine babies."

I stop in the hallway, jaw on my chest in amazement. "You have *nine* children?"

Maire beams with pride. "It's a miracle what the body can do when the government isn't messing with it. Yes, I have nine children of my very own and I nursed every one of them with my breasts. Tommy is the oldest." She grabs her chest with both hands and stands straight and tall. "Women are meant to have babies, my love. Not sweat our lives away in a factory or plant."

She starts down the hall again, her speech apparently over. I follow her, not sure how I feel about the whole thing. Having nine children is an amazing feat, but I also know woman can do so many things besides just having babies. I've only known Maire for a very little while, and I can already tell that she does much more than give birth to keep her mountain home running. Perhaps being a mother is the role she prizes the most.

I'm still considering this revolutionary idea when Maire stops and gestures down a righthand side corridor. "Here ya go." I can hear the sound of rushing water as I step in front of her and walk cautiously down the dimly lit, sloping passage until it opens into another great room. Maire follows me.

The floors are smooth white tile, like the main hall, but the ceiling and walls are still rough stone and soar at least thirty feet over my head. The air is thick with steam, the walls glistening and dripping condensation. A wide channel of water cuts across the middle of the floor, and arms of steam reach up from its surface to join the mists in the air. A stone bridge spans the gap. On the far side of the bridge, women and children and a few men are washing laundry in large tubs lined up along the river's edge. On the near side protruding knee-height from the rock floor, circular baths have been constructed with smooth rocks and sealed with mortar. Each is large enough to fit three or four bathers. Women with large jugs are filling the tubs from the river while others stand by faucets that gush steaming water. An opening at the apex of the room lets the majority of the steam escape, presumably to the outside.

"I suppose even if the Leaders decided to attack, you're in a pretty good spot to defend yourselves," I say.

"Very true. They don't know how to get past our guards and they wouldn't know what to do once they got in here anyhow. As far as we know, no one has ever mapped the place." I wonder about her assumption, and before I think twice, I open my mind and focus on maps of mines. Information flows through my conscious from all over the globe and throughout history, but there is nothing readily appearing of this place.

"That's your bath there." She points to the tub closest to us. Steaming water pours from a spigot into the smooth, white interior. "There's soap on the edge," she continues, "and you've got your towel and a robe. Do you need help scrubbing your hair?" She regards my head with interest. "You seem to have quite a bit of it."

"No." I touch my braid self-consciously. No one has washed my hair since I was a very small child, unable to do it myself, and even then, only Mother did it. "I'll be fine. Thank you."

She turns to walk away. "I'll be back for you soon. I've got to tend to a couple of naughty children."

I glance at the men working across the river, then at Maire's retreating back. "Maire?" I ask before she gets too far away. "Where do I get changed?" I pull at my dirty shirt.

She turns back to look at me in confusion until her face breaks into a smile and she chuckles. "Oh, dear. I quite forgot you flatlanders don't ever see each other naked except on the spy cameras. Okay then, just climb in the tub, clothes and all. They need to be washed anyway. Adelaide will help ya out with the robe and no one will be the wiser."

I don't quite believe her, and she can tell.

"They'll only see your head, dearie, unless they're right next to the tub lookin' in, and they're all busy. Even if they could, they probably wouldn't care. We're not as modest as the lot of you down there. Naked girls are old news. Now get going before your water cools off and you catch your death of cold." She looks beyond me and says, "Adelaide, hurry up. You've got to get back to the kiddos when you're finished here." With that she vanishes down the passageway from where we came.

I hear a splash and turn to see a girl about my age with short brown hair walk up and sit at the faucet controls of my tub. She is very thin with dark eyes and a yellow shirt and green skirt. She tests the water in the bath with her hand, turns the water off, and scowls when she sees me staring at her.

I look down at my filthy clothes and decide Maire is probably right. I do need a good scrubbing, and the men probably can't see over the edge of the tub. But this girl can. I hesitate, looking at her a bit too long before I reach down to take my shoes off. She rolls her eyes and folds her arms.

If this is how they live underground, then this is what I'm going to have to get used to. I set my boots by the rock wall surrounding the large basin. I place the towel and robe next to it.

Stairs lead into the depths of the smoothed hole. I start to pull my socks off then stop. They need to be washed as well.

Tentative steps down into the bath immerse my feet, then calves, then knees in the slightly steaming water. It's just the right temperature—hot enough to turn my skin red, but not scalding. I inch in farther as my body becomes accustomed to the heat, and soon I'm standing on the bottom, the water reaching my armpits. Peeling my wet clothes off under water proves to be harder than I thought. The girl with the short brown hair continues to stand by the faucet, only now she stares across the river at the people doing their wash. I try smiling at her to see if she is noticing my struggle, but she doesn't notice.

After wrestling my clinging shirt over my head, I add it to the pile of wet, dirty clothes on the side of the rocks next to a small brick of soap left by another bather. I decide keeping my back to the girl is the best policy, even though my front is facing the people on the other side of the underground river. I scrub discretely with the soap, slight indentations from fingerprints dotting its smooth sides. Still, it smells nice and feels so good to lather my hair and scrub the grime of prison life away.

After two full-body scrub downs, I hold my breath and dunk under the water, rinsing the soap from my hair and a part of my past from my heart. I emerge feeling invigorated and almost excited.

"He's not yours, you know."

The loud voice startles me and I splash water out of the tub in my hurry to fold my arms over my chest. I sink into the water up to my neck and lock eyes with the girl still perched on the edge of my bath. I can't help but wish the already murky water was a bit dirtier, so she couldn't see me.

"Excuse me?" I say.

"Thomas. He's not yours." There is no warmth or friend-ship in her eyes, only mistrust— and something else.

"I never said he was. I didn't say anything at all."

"Doesn't matter. You can't just trot in here with your flat-landing ways and gobs of long hair and take our men, especially not our Thomas. He's got a future planned, you know. He's got a girl just about to be assigned to him, and you aren't her."

I'm not sure how to react. Part of me is hurt and confused. I hadn't thought Thomas was *mine,* but I also hadn't thought about him belonging to anyone else. I haven't had time to think past survival in so long. I'm not sure I know how.

I can't help it—I touch my lips with one fingertip, thinking about our last kiss. Where is he now?

The girl turns away from me, and a moment later Maire re-appears at the cavern entrance. Her round body wobbles down the slope like she might topple and roll at any moment, but she doesn't. "Ya still in there, lass? I thought Adelaide woulda helped you out by now. Well, no matter." She opens the robe and holds it up, looking purposefully away from the tub. "Here ya go, lassie."

I look at the girl with the short hair. She's staring at me

again but turns with a sniff to look at the people across the river. None of them are looking my way, so I step out of the tub and down the stairs, into the embrace of the robe. The cooler air makes goosebumps stand up all over my skin.

"Thank you," I whisper.

There is no privacy, and heaven only knows what was in that water, but compared to Secondary School's cold, hard shower stalls and the synthesized voice directing me, Maire's strong arms wrapping a rough cotton robe around my wet skin feel perfect.

"Aw, it's nothing. Let's go." She turns to the girl. "Thank you, Adelaide—you're done here, lass. Take her things over to the washers and go back to your students."

Adelaide—I have to remember that. She doesn't like me and I know by now to keep track of who's on your side and who's not.

"Yes, Ma."

"Ma? Is that short for Maire?" I ask as we make our way back up the slope to the exit.

"Naw, love, it's short for mama."

"Mama? What does that mean?" There are so many strange new words and customs here I wonder how long it will take me to learn them all.

Maire laughs and looks at me sideways. "Mother, dear. It's short for mother. Adelaide is my daughter. I know you must have mothers down there in the cities."

*Oh no,* I think. *Adelaide is Thomas's sister.* Then out loud, "Yes, we do. Er... I mean, I did. She died."

Maire's head tips to one side and before I know it, she pulls me into another crushing embrace. "You poor thing. What haven't you been through."

At first, I stiffen, not used to public affection, or any affection, really. But her arms feel like everything I've been missing and then some. I melt into them, take a deep breath, and hug her back.

# SEVEN

"**G**et those clothes on and let's get hopping. The whole mine is buzzing about a flatlander living with us." Maire's voice is kind, but I can tell she is in a hurry.

"All right." I look at the simple yellow skirt and bright blue shirt laid on the bed, so different from regulation uniforms. The few hours I've been awake among these mountain people have already changed my perspective. I find my hesitation about wearing colorful clothing has turned to anticipation. I can't wait to get them on.

"I'll be just the other side." She leaves, closing the large wooden door behind her.

I look around for the autoeye out of habit. All that meets my gaze are smooth rock walls. I let the robe fall to the floor and put on the soft under things and clothing. They are a good fit and I feel a thrill of delight and confidence run through me as I examine the beautiful colors. Soft brown leather shoes are set by the door for me. They are a bit tight, but the leather is made to stretch. They hug my feet in a very reassuring way.

I open the door and give a sheepish grin to Maire.

"Ahh! That blue suits ya. Brings out the green in your eyes." She smiles, then picks up a strand of my tangled wet hair. "What we going to do with this now, eh?"

I take the strand back and push it over my shoulders, tucking the sides behind my ears. The blue fabric fills me with a boldness I haven't felt in a very long time.

"I'll keep it just as it is, thank you." As much as I want to fit in with the rest of these people, one of my fondest memories is of Mother brushing my hair and whispering stories to me. I don't think I'll ever be able to cut it.

I expect Maire to put her hands on her hips and reprimand me, but instead she gives me a comb carved from wood and embellished with a flower design and says, "Suit yourself. At least pull the snarls out while we walk down the way. It's time you got your work assignment." Then to herself, "Never seen a girl with so much hair."

I admire the workmanship of the comb for a minute then yank it through my hair, loving the way it feels hanging loose on my back instead of in a tight braid for school or the dirty knots that developed in prison. The soft shoes make my footsteps almost soundless, and I note that Maire wears the same type. Only her huffing and puffing keep her progress from being unheard.

The tunnels are so confusing. Everything looks the same except the main shaft connecting the wash room and most of Thomas's family quarters.

I try to memorize the series of turns and straightaways that lead us to the massive tiled room I passed out in the day before. A group of people are milling about, sipping drinks and chatting. I look for Thomas but don't see him. An older man approaches Maire and I, smiling.

"You must be Imani." He has twinkling gray eyes and white hair with black flecks. His face is covered in a matching beard. I've never seen a grown man with facial hair—it isn't considered useful in the cities. I think about Thomas and his prison beard, rough and unkempt. This man's is trimmed, sculpted even, with sharp lines cutting across his lower cheeks.

"Yes." I smile back and nod.

"That's wonderful. I'm Joe Finnis."

"Joe's in charge around here," Maire says. "He's our leader but not like the Leaders out there." She thumbs at the exit door. "Much more fun."

Joe smiles. "I'm not sure I'd go that far. We would like to put you right to work if you're up to it. Thomas has told us a lot about you." He speaks with a different accent than the others. I feel self-conscious about what Thomas might have told them.

"Don't worry," Joe says, reading my unease. "It was all good. How do you feel about teaching a class or two to the youngsters around here?"

I imagined him handing me a pickax and telling me to hit the tunnels. His suggestion catches me off guard. "You want me to teach?"

"You've got more schooling than most of our children. Plus, the adults would like to know what it's really like living out in the towns these days."

"You want me to teach adults and children?" I'm on the verge of being offended. Teachers are evil. They labeled me as Neurodeficient as a child because I cried when song birds were destroyed. They were always so quick to point out my emotional flaws and sit me in front of the class as an example. Every teacher I had punished me for being myself. I'd never met one I liked. Professor789 and his cruel words and double agenda still make me shudder. The teacher at Secondary School who happily vaporized a yellow songbird fills me with disgust.

But just like the clothes and accent, everything down here is different. Joe doesn't mean to say he thinks I'd fit in well as the type of teacher I'm familiar with. Maybe teachers are nice here. I can scarcely imagine it.

Joe is studying my face. I wonder how much of my thoughts have run across it for the world to read. His eyebrows raise in questioning arches when I don't give an answer so he adds, "Only after we clear up a few things, and only if you feel up to it."

Maire comes to my rescue. "She's been through a lot, Joe. She might want to hold off a few days."

"Of course. It's just that we're in the middle of a few things on the outside, and her information might be able to help us," Joe says.

"What would I have to do, exactly?" I ask.

Joe scratches his beard and looks at me thoughtfully. "Why don't we start with some questions from the elders? Do you think you could do that? We'd just be sitting down at a table here and chatting."

"I guess so." I shrug and look around the room, suddenly aware of several people watching me.

"Good. Let's get started then." He claps his hands and calls the room to attention. "Please be seated if you are here for the council meeting. If you are not invited to the council meeting, please leave." His voice is friendly, but there is an undertone of authority that suggests I should probably avoid his bad side.

A group of older folks, including Maire and Joe, start pulling out chairs and sitting down, arms crossed and eyes on me. Joe motions me to a seat on one side of the table and calls for the doors to the room to be shut.

This feels like a lot more than a quick chat or a job assignment. The people aren't all friendly looking, some scowling, some with arms folded, eyes down. Even Maire seems a bit aloof in this setting, her face solemn as a stone.

When the doors are closed and everyone is seated, Joe clears his throat. "Now that we're all here and settled, how about you tell us what you're really doing down here."

His conversational tone makes me unsure if I heard him correctly. "Excuse me?"

Another man speaks up. "No one gets away from the Leaders twice. Once, maybe, if you're lucky, and our Thomas is definitely a lucky bugger. But you've escaped twice. That just doesn't happen. And how did you get from the prison to the center without being wiped? The story just doesn't add up."

I sit back in my chair and defensively fold my arms across my chest, mirroring the stance most of them have taken. "I'd heard rumors about a mountain colony and wanted to come here, but I didn't think it was real. When I met Thomas and he offered to help me escape and bring me here..." I trail off when pain shoots through my head, followed by an explosion of facts.

*Escape 17790 Spring, infraction number 43. Mind Wipe recommended after debriefing.*

*Escape 82372 Autumn, infraction 33 and 90. Second attempt, recommended Mind Wipe.*

*Escape 92278 Autumn, infraction 12. Previous attempts successful at evasion, hunt at all costs.*

"Enough!" I rub my temples, eyes closed. The bump from my fall is a hard, hot lump, and it hurts when I touch it. I tip my head forward until it touches the table, and I focus on the moment, on not hearing the information, and hopefully on not looking like a total lunatic.

A hand on my back startles me, and I glance to the side to see Maire watching me with worried eyes.

"Enough is right. Maybe she did get wiped. How do we

know any different?" a male voice asks.

"Ernest," Maire says, her voice serious. "You've seen them. They don't have no life behind their eyes. They walk around with their arms lolling... it ain't natural. This lass has been through some trauma is all."

"But what are those traumas? And how much damage— what kind of damage—did they do? That's what we want to know," Joe says.

Head throbbing, I can't understand why they're concerned. I'm a teenage girl who hates the Leaders. "They let me go," I finally say, hoping the truth will stop the argument while I continue to press on my aching temples.

"That's a lie." The man named Ernest jumps out of his chair at my words. "She's prolly got a tracker on her, prolly a spy. They don't just *let people go*."

"They know exactly where we are." It was Joe's turn to quiet him down. "No need to track us. As for being a spy, well, we all know how difficult that would be. Can't radio anything out of these stone walls, and we're going to know if she slips out to meet anyone." A few dark chuckles circle the room.

"But she's been to the lower entrance," Ernest says. "They didn't know about that."

"And they still don't. Our men took care of the trackers that followed them," Joe says.

Ernest sits back down, looking defeated.

"Why don't you just tell us what you can remember," Joe

says. He is getting less and less friendly by the minute.

I decide to try again, though the situation is so complicated I don't know where to start or which details will be important to these people. "I was in prison. Thomas and I tried to escape. Thomas got away, and I got shot. I woke up in the Institute, Hamen's base, and saw Thomas outside my window. I told the guards I wanted to go for a walk and found Thomas hiding in the woods. The guards chased us, but we got away."

"You told the guards you wanted to go for a walk?" one man asks, eyebrows raised.

"You got shot and then just woke up in the Institute?" a woman questions.

Joe shakes his head. "None of this makes sense. What were you in prison for in the first place? People don't just walk out of prison."

Other people shout questions and doubts, and I panic. Maybe being honest wasn't the best idea. Hasn't Thomas told them anything? How much should I tell them? I trust Thomas, but these people don't seem like him. They can't be worse than the Leaders, but after Hamen's betrayal, that doesn't mean much.

A new terrifying thought dawns on me. What if they found out I had every last bit of information from the outside world jammed in my head? I already know they want to know more about my world—Joe said he wanted me to teach adults about it. If they realize just how much information I have, who knows what they'd do to access it.

I stand up as the rapid-fire questions continue. I want to run back to the safety of my tiny bedroom with the soft bed and beautiful quilt. Or better yet, the forest with the blue sky and birds. Even my sterile gray sleep pod back home would be better than this barrage.

My eyes dart around the room, noting the location of doors and position of chairs, judging the best escape route. I must look like a trapped animal because Joe and Maire stand up too and each put a hand on my shoulders.

The sound of a door swinging open behind me has me turning, and relief floods my chest as Thomas walks in. I focus on his face and take deep breaths. He walks straight for me and I can't help but shake off the hands holding me and walk to him.

We throw our arms around each other in an embrace that silences the whole room. Tears trickle down my cheeks, taking bits and pieces of the pressure in my heart with them.

"Thomas," I whisper. "Where have you been?"

He pulls back and looks at me, eyes full of concern. "I'll explain later." Then he faces Joe. "What's going on?"

"That's what we'd like to know, Thomas," Joe says.

"Tommy?" Maire looks at him, questioning our closeness in the way only a mother can.

"I can answer all the questions ya need. Imani and I met in the prison. I got her out, but not before they messed her up good with some weird new program they've got going on in there. She needs time and space, and she's not here to bugger us up."

Got it?"

"I don't appreciate your tone." Ernest is at the edge of his seat.

"I don't appreciate the way you're treating our guest," Thomas says.

"Thomas, you don't know her very well, son." Joe sits back down. "Why don't you join us and we'll sort this out and decide where to go from here."

Thomas makes a low exasperated groaning noise in the back of his throat, and then I feel his arms relax a bit. He leans in and whispers in my ear, "Just play along and we'll get out of here soon enough."

I nod and let him steer me back to my seat. He pulls a new chair up beside me and reaches out to take my hand. He is so warm, so strong. His hands are rough and callused, leaving no question of their capability in any situation. I begin to relax a bit.

Maire does not relax. "Thomas, I'd like you to first explain this." She motions to our locked hands on my lap. "You've been promised to Alice." Her voice seems to break just the slightest.

Thomas takes a big breath before he speaks. "Alice will have to get over it."

"Thomas!" Maire practically squawks as a murmur ripples through the group of older men and women.

I squeeze his hand again and he squeezes back.

Joe clears his throat. "I don't think that's such a wise declaration, son."

"I'm tired of your *wisdom*. I want to pick my own girl, and I pick Imani."

"But you don't know her..." Maire trails off, a tear actually trickling down her rock-hard expression.

Thomas looks at me, eyes soft, then back at his mother. "I do know her. Forgive me, Ma, but you don't know what you're talking about."

Maire sets her jaw. "If you know her so well, then tell me this: Why would the Leaders send soldiers to get her back with the express instructions to *bring her back alive at all costs*? And why would they then add to the retrieval crew an emissary—the next day, no less—with messengers saying that she is to return to the Institute immediately if she ever wants to see her mother alive again?"

She's looking at me by the end of her little speech, so my shock and confusion are evident. What is she talking about? I look to Thomas to see if he knows anything about this. He stares at his mother with narrowed eyes, anger plain on his features. It hits me like a blow to the chest. I don't want to be a wedge between Thomas and his family, especially for something that isn't true.

I meet Maire's eyes. "My mother is dead," I declare firmly.

"Not according to one Mr. Hamen, who apparently has a great deal to lose if he loses you," Joe says. "He sent a photograph and a letter with his soldiers." He takes a piece of paper out of his coat pocket and hands it to me. It is an envelope stamped with a blue spider. Inside is a small piece of paper with a brief note written in a blocky hand.

> *This wasn't part of the deal, Imani. Return to us immediately and I'll make sure she is here to welcome you.*
>
> *Hamen*

A black-and-white photograph slips into my hands. My mother, just as I remember her, sits on the edge of a bed, clearly in the Institute, wearing a white smock. She looks healthy, her hair is brushed and smooth, and a smile plays on her lips.

She is alive.

**EIGHT**

"**I** think there's a bit more to this story than what you're telling us, Imani." Joe's voice is steady and calm, the complete opposite of my heart. "Have a seat and let's figure this out."

"Is that really your mum?" Thomas asks.

I can't breathe. I can't sit down. Every muscle in my body is rigid. Everything inside me threatens to leak out.

"Imani?" Thomas asks again.

"Yes. It's her," I manage. "That's the room they held me in at the Institute—or one just like it." It's hard to speak. I can't look away from the picture.

"But she died at your home? You were with her in the last, weren't ya? How could she be alive and smiling up here with the wackos?"

"I don't know." I can barely get the answer out. I sit back in my chair and study the photograph, looking for any hint of falsehood.

There is nothing to doubt. Her face has aged a bit, but it is her—the same soft smile and long dark hair, just like mine. She is alive. Not only that, but she is with Hamen, and she seems happy.

I can't process any of this. I had been in that very building. I just missed her. What if she was waiting for me at lunch the day I left? What if I would have gone with Hamen? Would I be sitting by her side in this photo, smiling as well?

Tears burn my eyes and drip down my cheeks. I suck in a hiccup of air.

"Imani, it's okay." Thomas's arm is around me. "This has to be a trick. He's a shifty, shady guy—nothing is out of his power. Even hurting you like this, even making a dead woman look alive in a photo. But why would he do this? Why does he want you back so bad?"

Thomas may think the photo is fake, but I know in my heart it's real. Mother is alive. Hamen wants me back because of all the information he piled into my brain, and he knew exactly how to get me to cooperate.

"Speak up, girl. Answer our questions," a man to my left says.

"I have to go back." It comes out as a whisper.

"Don't be foolish, child." Maire's tone is more patient now, but I can tell she is just as confused as the rest of them. "Tell us what happened and let us help ya."

"Why do they want you to come back?" Joe asks, echoing Thomas's question.

"I wasn't there," I manage to say a bit louder.

"Wasn't where, Imani?" Thomas is still holding me.

"When she died, I wasn't with her. I never saw…" I take a deep breath, wipe my eyes, and try to calm the sob that is still threatening my throat. "The Leaders sent two men to come and take her to the Shop in town."

"The Shop?" Maire asks.

"Where people go for their final rest." The words catch, but I get them out and take another deep breath. I can still see the large building in the center of town where people went in and boxes of ashes came out. It was a constant reminder of what we had waiting for us when the Leaders decided our life was done.

"So they took your mom away and told you she was dead?" a woman to the right of me asks.

I nod.

"Then what happened?"

"Then I went to Secondary School." I think about the day we lowered her body's ashes into the ground at the Field of Yesterday. What had been in that box? Where had she been all this time? Did she know I had been in prison? Does she know where I am now?

A man in the back of the group sighs noisily. "I don't have time for this. I've got folks to oversee today. We need to come up with a plan."

Thomas speaks loudly for me. "Then her lousy brother got her thrown in prison and she was taken to the Institute when we tried to escape. Now she's here."

"Is that true?" Joe asks me.

"Yes." I nod.

"What got you thrown in prison?" Joe asks.

"I found films and music in the archives at Secondary School and I broadcasted them to the whole school."

A murmur ripples through the room as people turn and whisper to each other. I look up from the photo to scan their faces. Some are laughing and some look concerned.

"No wonder he wants you back." Joe shakes his head and rubs his eyes as if massaging a headache.

"What do you mean?" I ask.

"You don't like the Leaders, you poked around in the archives, and you spread it to others. You're like a walking illegal info-bomb. Biological warfare at the information level. Brilliant, really. No wonder he's terrified." He rubs his chin, examining me. "What all did you read in the archives?"

As soon as he stops talking, a short burst of pain precedes my mind wheeling through examples of biological warfare. Gruesome images shuttle past my closed eyelids, and I force them open and take a deep breath. "I mostly found music and films, like I said. But at the Institute..." I shake my head, unsure of how to explain what was forced inside. "I know it all now."

"What do you mean?" Joe asks.

"Everything the Leaders have hidden from us—I have all of it." I tap my head with a finger.

Thomas tightens his grip on my shoulders. "Imani, hold on,

dearie. What do you mean, you have all of it?"

Maire hands me a handkerchief from one of her pockets. It is clean and soft, bright white. It makes me think of the gray one with the blue spider Mother showed me before she died. But she didn't die. She is alive.

"Imani?" Thomas asks again quietly.

I take a deep breath, looking up from the handkerchief. Everyone is watching me. "Hamen didn't put me through the Mind Wipe. He filled my mind with all the archived information from old earth. I have it *all*. Art, music, poetry, science, mathematics—you name it, it's in my brain. I don't know how he did it, but he's been using the Mind Wipe program as a cover for his revolution." Murmurs sweep through the room, but I keep going. "He said he wants to plant the information in everyone he can and overthrow the government peacefully, through sharing information, and he wanted my help."

I don't know what I expect as a response, but the silence that follows isn't it. I search the faces around me but am met with blank stares. Only Thomas squeezes my hand in comfort.

"I didn't help him." I start to feel a bit panicked by their lack of reaction. "I left, with Thomas. I couldn't stay there. He wanted me to pretend I was someone else..."

Joe holds up a hand to silence me and looks at a man across from him. They nod at each other, and then Joe says, "Imani, this changes our plans entirely."

"It certainly does," the loud man at the back shouts. "She's a walking wiper is what she is. You've seen the nutters they turn out of that place. Once their brains have been messed around with, they wander the fields, drooling down their own faces and attacking anyone who goes near. It's an evil thing, I say. She'll be stumbling around here in no time. Then she'll keel over dead like the rest of them. It ain't natural. I say we let her go back. Get rid of her in case it's contagious."

"That's enough," Joe says, glaring at the man. Then he looks at me, and I think I see a glimmer of compassion or sympathy. "Imani, we can't let you go back. It's not safe. I think Thomas is right and this is a trick. Who knows what he'll do once he has you back."

I shake my head. "I know my mother. That's her. And I know that room."

"Is there any chance she was there before she died? Could she have traveled there to visit him then returned?" Joe says.

His solution only takes a moment of thought to disprove. "No, it's too far from our pod. We lived in the lumber regions to the southwest. She was never gone long enough for a journey like this. She was always there when I got home from lessons."

Joe looks around the circle and a few men nod. Then Joe's attention is on me again. "All right, Imani. If your mother is really there, we'll get word to her that you are with us and we'll figure something out—a plan to free her without putting you in danger's way. In the meantime, we carry on as planned. Marcus, can you call in James and Peter?"

A man in the back, one of the ones who had nodded at Joe a moment ago, stands up and walks out of the room.

At my questioning look, Joe explains, "Peter and James are our best spies. They will be able to check out Hamen's claim. If your mother is being held against her will, they will help us figure out a way to get her out. If they can't find her or anyone else who matches her description, well, let's just see what happens."

"No," I say, fear rising in my gut at the risk these two are taking for me and my mother. "I can't let you do that. You don't know Hamen. He'll kill them or wipe them if he catches them. I can walk right into the Institute and be with her and make a plan from there. I've beat them twice. I can beat them again."

Joe is shaking his head. "Imani, that's ridiculous. You can't go back there. He'll wipe you fast as a whistle." Thomas lets his arm fall from behind my chair, leaving a cold stripe across my shoulders.

"But it doesn't make sense any other way. The whole reason I'm here is because of her, and too many people have been hurt because of me already. I'm not going to risk your two men. I need to take care of this myself." I point at the note. "He's not going to wipe me. I'm a huge asset. He has plans for me, which means I'll be safe." I know this is the best option, even as my heart aches to think of leaving Thomas and this mountain haven as soon as I discovered it. As confident as I sound, I know it would be a huge risk to go back to the Institute. But the chance to see Mother makes it worth it.

Joe's already shaking his head. "We have been fighting these folks for quite a while. We know what we're doing. We're more efficient; we have weapons and experience. You wouldn't even know how to get up the river."

"I can figure it out. I'm not completely helpless," I say.

The man named Marcus returns with two large men following him. They are dressed in clothing the same color as the trees, mottled greens and browns. One has a thick scar crossing his cheek. They look older than Thomas and me but not old enough to be Leaders. Large black shock rifles hang across their broad backs.

Joe stands. "Thank you, Marcus. I'll bring them up to date." He reaches toward me. "Can I show them the photograph?"

I hold my smiling mother to my chest, feeling the situation spin beyond my control. "There's no need. Really. You don't need to get involved," I protest.

"Imani, we need you here as much as they need you there. Information is a valuable asset in this conflict. Stay here and share what you have with us. Help us fortify our defenses and teach us everything you can, and I'll do everything I can to make sure your mother gets out alive," Joe says.

His fervor beats against my conviction, and I look at Thomas. He nods, agreeing with Joe.

"Imani, don't go back there. You can't trust Hamen. Let the boys here suss it out." He tucks a strand of my hair behind my ear. "You don't have to do everything alone anymore. Let us help you."

Behind him, I see Maire nod. I hesitate as Thomas's words sink in. A weight feels lifted from my shoulders when I let myself believe him. I don't have to do this by myself. I can trust Thomas, at least, and he trusts these people. I slowly stretch out my arm, giving Joe the picture.

"Don't worry, we'll give it back to you." Joe smiles. "This is the best option for you and your mother. Trust me."

*Trust him.* The words echo in my mind.

"He's right." Thomas puts his hand back on my shoulder. His eyes are clear and bright over his sad smile.

"Okay," I say, and I hope I'm right.

# NINE

fter everything is settled, Thomas and Maire return to their assignments. Thomas tells me briefly they've been keeping him busy in the mines—he's one of their better mineral testers and they would work him every shift if they could. He gives me a swift kiss and a promise to see me soon before striding out as quickly as he came. Maire, still kind, is notably distant after Thomas's revelation about us having some sort of claim on each other. I watch her walk down the passageway after a farewell nod to me and wonder if she will come back around or if I've just lost an ally.

Thomas had explained to me on the boat that the mountain people govern themselves aside from the Leaders. Sitting in on the council meeting, I learn that Joe is essentially in charge, but he listens to the comity of elders and they vote on big decisions. Each elder is in charge of a different aspect of mountain life.

After the meeting, Joe introduces me to Minerva, the elder in charge of education. She is a short woman, stout, but not as heavy as Maire. She walks with her back straight and shoulders stiff. Her hair is cropped shorter than most of the other women and her face is tight. Lines around her eyes and mouth and gray flecks in her spiky hair make her look old. She wears browns and grays that match her hair instead of the bright colors most of the mountain people wear.

On the way to the second level classrooms, we pass dormitories for single people and living quarters for families, many bustling with people at work on different projects and tasks— whitewashing the walls, sweeping the floors, repairing lights. One woman paints a colorful design on a door.

Between Minerva's running monologue on the school system and what I observe, the shape of mountain life begins to form in my mind. Mountain families live together, rollicking with as many children as they want. Young ones don't have to work. They attend classes and play in the common rooms with all manner of handmade toys and games. They fill the halls of the second level with laughter and movement. They remind me of birds flitting through the forests, too fast for anyone to catch. The children in my home community stood in gray smocks and tunics, perfect lines, hands at their sides, faces somber and futures determined by a test and a group of Leaders who never met them. These little ones are all wild cards. They can be anyone and anything now or when they grow up. The energy is intoxicating. I wonder what I would have been like had I been raised in a place like this.

Minerva leads me past door after door of brightly colored rooms full of small bodies, songs, and chatter.

"We have the children divided by ages for most classes, and by ability, and by interest. You'll be working with Adelaide in the history and storytelling classes. These are new disciplines since we moved into the mines. Once the Leaders raided our village, we decided it was time to start teaching the young ones about their past. Now that you're here, hopefully they will get a clearer vision of where we all came from."

"History is written by survivors," I say to myself.

"What's that?" Minerva asks, narrowing her eyes.

"Nothing," I say.

She's a severe woman. She smiles frequently at people we pass, but it doesn't reach her eyes. She knows everyone, and I can tell she's respected but not liked by the way people straighten up when we walk past. Even the children grow quiet and watch her.

"You mentioned Adelaide. Did you mean Thomas's sister?"

"Yes. Have you met?" Minerva says.

"Yes," I say, trying to hide a cringe.

"Excellent. She's dependable and good at engaging the children without resorting to tricks and bribes."

"I'll bet she is," I mutter.

We turn a corner into a new classroom, and the thin brown-haired girl from the baths is standing there, wearing a brown shirt and orange trousers with green patches on the knees instead of a skirt. I've seen a few women dressed in pants, but not many. She's bent over a small one who is struggling to open a wooden box with a brightly colored outdoor scene painted on the sides.

"Let me help you, Joseph, and you can have it back." Adelaide's voice is calm and reassuring. The little boy looks up at her, reluctant to hand over his prize, but at her smile, he relents.

"That's a good boy, Joseph," Minerva says and both of them look up at us.

Adelaide's patient smile melts into a scowl when she sees me.

"Imani is going to help in your classes. She's going to take over story time each day and help you identify gaps in their historical knowledge," Minerva says.

Adelaide rolls her eyes. "That figures."

"Is there a problem?" Minerva asks. She looks between the two of us.

Adelaide slips the previously hidden latch on the box to one side, allowing it to open easily, and hands it to the little boy. He turns the box over on the ground and small green and blue glass balls roll out. He chases after them happily on his hands and knees, grabbing with chubby fingers and laughing.

Adelaide answers, "No. No problem." She folds her arms, takes a step back, and looks at my right shoulder as she addresses me. "We have twenty-five young ones and they have already had their lesson for the day. Middle grade classes are coming in next. There are about forty of them, but teachers on my shift have to help with elimination training and clean up first."

"What's elimination training?" I ask.

"Changing diapers, washroom lessons. The basics of poop." Adelaide smiles as she says this.

"I've never changed a diaper before," I say. "We had nannies for those things in my community."

"You'll be fine at it," Adelaide says. "I'll make sure you get plenty of practice."

"I'm leaving you in good hands," Minerva says. "Adelaide, make sure she can find her way back after lessons are finished."

"Yes, ma'am."

"What do you want me to teach them?" I ask Minerva before she strides away. I thought she'd direct me some, but she has barely mentioned more than the topic I am to teach. Now that we're in the classroom, I realize how totally I am out of my element. I have never spent time with children younger than me. I've never been in charge of anyone else. I never dreamed I would be. Back home in my community, I was sure I would be assigned to work in the sewers. Adelaide's obvious dislike makes it all ten times harder.

Minerva cocks her head. "Spend today getting to know the routine and the kids, make some notes and tomorrow start at the beginning. We want them to learn where we came from, how things work in the flat lands, and why it is that way."

Minerva marches out the door and the room loses part of its chill. I hadn't realized how anxious her presence made me. Adelaide's disdainful glare doesn't allow me to feel completely at ease, but the sight and sound of children laughing and playing warms my heart and distracts me from thinking about Mother.

The morning is spent mostly with young ones. I listen to Adelaide tell two groups a fanciful story about a girl delivering food to an elderly woman in the woods only to find that the woman has been eaten by a wolf. I worry that this will scare them—they are all around six years old—but they stare with wide eyes then cheer when the young girl cuts the wolf open, saving the old woman from its stomach. A bolt of pain warns me before the story brings up an implanted memory with slight variations: *Little Red Riding Hood*. I make a note to myself—they will probably be okay hearing about the wars.

We eat our midday meal with the students in another large tiled room. Although not as big as the room on the main floor where everyone gathers, sun pipes capped with thick glass in the ceiling allow natural light to pass through the rock and fill the common area with sunshine. Large wooden boxes filled with dirt and plants of all types thrive from a combination of sun and artificial lamps. There are green tomatoes clinging to stout little bushes, neat rows of spinach and carrot greens alongside what could be radishes. A second container is filled with huge zucchini plants, and a third houses what appears to be sweet potato vines. There are fruit trees, apricot and plum, lemon and fig, in giant pots along the walls. In the center of the room, a large container holds flowers of varying heights and colors. At the far end of the space, a series of bars have been erected in a grid formation, almost like scaffolding. Children climb all over it, laughing and swinging.

*Jungle gym*, I think, and painful flashes of similar scenes, only outdoors, fill my mind. I used to love climbing trees when I could get away to do it. This looks like so much more fun. Jealousy and excitement fill my heart.

Adelaide stands in front of me in line for food but after choosing her meal, she finds her way to a table with other girls and boys our age. I don't mind. I need a break from her scowls and hostility. I pick my own bowl of stew and piece of bread. There is also milk to drink. I wonder where they keep their cows or if they ship it in. I sit at a table by myself and enjoy the salty goodness of the vegetables and broth while I watch the young ones play. A boy, probably around eleven years old, approaches me with his bowl and glass.

"Are you the lady from the flat lands?"

"Yes. Who are you?"

"I'm Jonas. Can I sit with you?"

"Of course."

He slides into the seat next to me and smiles, exposing crooked teeth and twinkling eyes surrounded by clusters of freckles. He takes a bit bite of bread then starts talking with his mouth full, crusts turning into mash as he speaks.

"I heard you're going to be teaching us history," he says.

"That's right," I say, leaning over my bowl as I bring another bite of soup to my mouth.

"Have you been to the capital? How many Leaders have you met? Do you know anyone who's had the Mind Wipe?"

In his pause to take another bite, I take a breath to answer his questions—which reveal just how little he and the rest of the children know about life in the flat lands—but he continues before I have a chance, big eyes focused on me and mouth wide open as he chomps on his bread between words.

"Do they really spy on everything you do all day, every day? Like, even going to the bathroom?" His eyes are huge as he asks this last question.

"Didn't you have autoeyes in your village above ground?" I ask.

"We had a couple in the center of town, but not everywhere, and they got broken during the raids."

"They have them in every home, but not every room," I say. "Bathrooms are off limits. That's where we go when we want to be alone or do something forbidden."

"Like *what*?" He is leaning in as close as he can without leaving his chair. I can tell he's expecting a really shocking answer, so I give it to him.

"Like hug your mom."

He sits back and screws up his nose. "That's illegal?"

"Yep."

"Wow. I hug my mom all the time. Can I bring my mom to your story time?"

"I don't know the rules down here. Is that illegal?"

"I dunno. I'll find out." At this he dives his spoon into the bowl of soup and takes a big slurp. His furrowed brow likely means he's thinking about what I've said.

Pretty soon a few more brave kids join us, some asking questions. One girl in a pink dress touches my hair, pulling it through her fingers, admiring the length. We are all laughing and talking by the time it's announced that we need to move to the next set of classes. A few of them follow me as I trail Adelaide. When we get back to our classroom, there is a man and a woman sitting in the back of the room.

"Can I help you?" Adelaide asks as the young ones file in and find their seats at the tables, chatting quietly.

"We came to hear the flatlander speak," the man says. "If that's all right."

"This class is for young ones. You'll have to set something up with the council if you want her to talk to you."

The man and woman exchange glances as Adelaide turns from them and starts setting up her materials for her lesson.

"I'm just observing today anyway," I add.

They smile and nod. "We'll talk to Minerva and be back tomorrow," the man says, and as he leaves, he looks back at me.

After completing ten years of schooling, each person in the community rotates through the main jobs until they find something they enjoy. Thomas completed his rotations before the raids and found he liked mineral identification, so he spends most of his time working in the lower level tunnels for the next few weeks. I see him that night on his way to the baths, covered in dust and sweat. We exchange smiles but that's all because of the throngs of people around us and because it's late. In the morning he meets me at my door accompanied by four young children. I step out of my room uncertainly, watched by four set of big eyes.

"This is Joey, Anna, Sariah, and Milo," Thomas says as he pats each child on the head. Upon closer inspection, I see one has Thomas's eyes, another his nose, and they all share his hair, both color and cut. They are his siblings. "The rest are already down there or running wild someplace else."

The introduction seems to break the ice for them, and they smile at me and chat amongst themselves conspiratorially as we walk down the corridor. At one point they pause and step aside, letting us walk past. I can hear them egging each other on.

"You do it!"

"No you!"

"Sally lost the draw, she has to do it."

I keep walking, letting my shoulder occasionally bump into Thomas's as we have our own conversation. Suddenly, a strong pull on a clump of my hair jerks my head back.

"Ow!" I cry and turn to catch the offender, but the four children stare back at me, faces solemn but eyes twinkling.

"Who did that?" Thomas says crossly.

The group of siblings giggle. The smallest girl, looking guilty and awestruck, speaks first.

"I'm sorry, Tommy. We just wanted to know if all that hair was really growing out of her head," she says, glancing at my head in amazement.

"Of course it is, you little fools." Thomas ruffles the little girl's hair in his large hand.

"You can just ask me next time. All right?" I rub my tingling scalp.

"Get your bums to breakfast and leave us be!" He runs toward them and they scatter, squealing, and run ahead of us down the tunnel. Thomas circles back to me and takes my hand.

"You okay?" he asks.

"Yes," I say. "My head is fine. Hair still attached."

"I meant with everything else," he says, studying me.

For the first time since seeing Thomas that morning, I remember my worries. I have no idea how to teach children and it seems that everyone has an opinion about my being in the mines, but I don't want to share my worries with Thomas in the few moments I have with him. He makes them feel unimportant.

"Yes," I say. "I'm really good. I love being here."

"I'm going to be extra busy down below. Ma will keep an eye out for you if you can't find me. Also Adelaide. She'll help you out."

I grimace. This is one worry I will share. "I don't think Adelaide likes me much," I confide.

"Why would you think that?" he asks with a cock of his head.

"Just a hunch." I sigh.

"She's feisty and loyal, but she's a good one. You can count on her."

We enter the cafeteria and get in line for our breakfast. I scan the crowd looking for people I know—mostly children from yesterday, but also the council members—quizzing myself on their names. Thomas's family is sitting together at a table in the far left. Adelaide is already eating so I grab my food quickly and sit with them. She is almost finished and I need to follow her to the classroom so I don't get lost. She gives me sideways glances as I sit with Thomas. I gulp my porridge and drink my milk quickly so she doesn't have to wait.

"Are you done yet?" she says as I put down my spoon and wipe my face on the inside hem of my long blue skirt like I've seen so many other girls do.

"Yep," I say and climb over the bench to join her.

"Hey, have fun up there," Thomas calls. I give him a tight smile.

"We're gonna have all the fun, Thomas," Adelaide answers and I'm pretty sure she's being sarcastic.

A pack of young ones follow us on our way to the classrooms. They are generally happy and loud, laughing, a moving rainbow of colors and smiles. A couple of Thomas's siblings are in the group, but they don't pay us any attention. There are adults moving with us to, but I don't pay them any attention. Others we pass in the hall stare at me. I'm still an oddity.

When we get to Adelaide's classroom, I'm surprised to see Minerva and a crowd of people waiting there for us. Adelaide opens the door after scanning the crowd with annoyed snort, and everyone pours into the room. Minerva catches my arm as I pass, and together we wait just outside the classroom until the hallway is clear.

"Good morning," Minerva says, the brightness of the greeting feeling forced. "We've had a surprising number of people express interest in listening to you speak to the young ones this morning. I spoke with the council, and they thought it would be beneficial for those not assigned to work duty at this time to be allowed to attend and learn about the rest of the society."

Her upturned nose makes it clear she disagrees with the council's decision, but I'm more concerned about talking in

front of this many adults. I nod in understanding even as my
stomach twists with nerves, and she gestures that I should enter
the room ahead of her. Adelaide is at the front, looking a little
overwhelmed as she helps the youngest find seats on the floor at
the front of the group. Many adults stand at the back. Some look
skeptical, sizing me up as I enter. I pretend not to notice. A bead
of sweat rolls down my neck, and I pretend that it's the stuffi-
ness of a room with too many bodies.

Minerva makes her way through the crowd to join Adelaide
at the front and claps to silence the low hum of the group.

"How lovely that so many are interested in Miss Imani's
stories." The disingenuous smile. "This is obviously more popular than we anticipated. Let's move to the common area." She
directs her gaze to two boys play wrestling. "Children, you will
not be permitted to play on the equipment while we are listening
to Miss Imani. You will take a seat at the tables. Feel free to sit
with your parents or siblings." She gestures a dismissal, and Adelaide begins to herd small ones back to the door.

Once everyone is settled in the large room with the plants, I
stand to the side while Adelaide makes a few announcements.
I'm so nervous I don't hear a word she says, and most people
seem to be looking at me rather than listening to her. Some of
the eyes seem friendly, and I decide to focus on them as I speak.

I turn when I feel someone touch my arm, and I see Adelaide, annoyed, telling me to go to the center and begin. Minerva
sits at the front center table, and I walk to stand in front of the

table next to hers. I won't be able to concentrate with Minerva looking at me with disapproval and judgment. Finding the smiling eyes, I take a deep breath.

"I know most of you haven't left the mountains in a long time. Maybe you never have. I'm going to do my best to help you understand what it's like down there, starting with my own experiences.

"I lived in a farming and lumber community far to the southwest of here. My mother worked in a textile mill and my father in the forests and lumber plant."

I describe our sleek white pods, so different from this primitive mine shaft adapted for habitation with plants and play equipment. I explain our job assignments, so foreign compared to their idea of finding work they enjoy. I talk about our schools, and at this point my words are flowing and I feel comfortable. Until I notice that only some of the adults are still paying attention. One man has his feet on the table and is quietly snoring. Minerva has a content smile.

I trail off mid-sentence and frown, thinking. "This all seems to be fairly boring to you. Does anyone have any questions they'd like me to answer?"

A sea of hands shoots up, the universal request to speak. I point at a small red-haired boy in the front row who is waving his arm frantically. "Yes?"

"Do you know any wipers? I heard there are wipers down there." A few of the adults laugh.

I shudder. "No, I don't know any wipers." *But I've been attacked by one.*

Next I pick a woman with kind eyes. "Yes?"

"I hear that you can only have two children. Is that true?" she asks.

"Yes, that is true. They have a formula for how much food the land can produce according to the population and made the law for baring children to match the necessary numbers."

"So, you only get one brother or sister? Ever?" a little boy blurts out. The adult next to him leans over and holds a finger to her lips.

"There are some very rare cases where a person has more than two, but usually just two or even just one."

I think about my own brother. I wonder where he is, if he has risen in the ranks of the Leaders or if he is still a cadet in a black uniform scanning hours and hours of autoeye recordings for any signs of disobedience. The little boy who asked the question shakes his head and the little girl next to him punches him in the shoulder.

"Don't get any ideas. I'm always gonna be your sister," she says.

I choose another young one.

"My dad says that down there you get nothing but leaves off the bushes to eat and that I'll have to go live down there if I don't behave myself," he says.

A chuckle rolls across the group, and I smile. After seeing

how they live, it would feel like a punishment to grow up as I did. "We had a lot of different things to eat, especially living in the farming communities. Our produce was fresh and there was plenty of it. We also had meat and eggs and milk. However, one of the punishments was food rationing. There were lots of times when others had full lunches and I had nothing because I was in trouble."

"That sounds mean," a little girl up front says.

"It's definitely mean," I say with a serious nod.

The crowd murmurs and Minerva raised her hand. "How long do you expect you'll stay here? What are your plans?" she asks before I can call on her. She tips her head as she speaks, as if it's an innocent question.

I nod at her and then turn to address the crowd. "While you can't see the flat lands from here, ever since I was a little girl I could see the mountains. My mother told me stories about the people who lived there. Most of it was rumors and none of it was as good as I could have imagined. I spent a lot of time trying to figure out a way to get here." I meet Minerva's eyes. "I don't ever want to leave."

Minerva makes a *hurmph* sound. Murmurs from the adults fill the room as they turn to one another.

"What did they tell you about us?" a boy with curly brown hair asks.

"That you have names instead of a number, that you got to pick your own jobs, and that you lived in tunnels underground,"

I say with a smile.

"That's all true!" the boy announces.

"And what if we don't want you here?" Adelaide calls over the growing noise. The crowd falls silent. I search her face for some sarcasm or humor in her words. There is none.

"I suppose that would be a problem," I say slowly.

Thomas's little sister Anna, sitting beside Adelaide, jumps up and shouts, "I want her here! I like her long hair. It's pretty. I wanna grown my hair out like that."

"Hush, Anna," Adelaide says, pulling her back into her seat.

"She tells good stories," declares the curly-haired boy.

The room fills with muttering and whispers.

"That's enough," Minerva calls over the crowd. "One more question, and then I'd like to hear more about the Secondary School."

From the forest of hands, I see one large hand and follow it down to Joe's face. How long has he been here? I feel brave, so I call on him. "Yes, Joe?"

"Were you betrothed in the flat lands? That is to say, how do they arrange partnerships down there?"

Faces turn to me in interest, and I purse my lips in thought. There is something more beneath his inquiry that makes me feel uneasy. His gaze lingers on me, but not my eyes. It makes me cringe.

"No, I wasn't. I am too young to be betrothed." I avoid looking at him. "They rank you according to your aptitude and achievement in secondary school or coming of age tests and pair you with a suitable companion."

"I supposed they don't put as much emphasis on family and procreation as we do," Joe says.

"I suppose not," I say and focus on the children who are eagerly awaiting my next story.

# ELEVEN

The days pass quickly. I'm kept busy with new tasks in the school rooms, speaking to anyone who wants to ask questions during an open discussion hour once a day. I learn as much about the mountains from their questions and reactions as they learn about the flat lands from my answers. I'm starting to get the hang of addressing the large groups that show up to listen, and I have the basic history of our society and where it's heading down to a quick presentation I can easily retell without getting flustered.

Thomas's work assignments and family chores mean we only see each other nights and mornings, usually for breakfast. I am still in my original room in his family's wing. Even though it is small and dimly lit, much like my cell, I like it. The warm, soft bed, frequent visitors, and ability to leave anytime I want makes all the difference. I wonder if Maire has told Thomas that he isn't allowed to be alone with me. There is always a swarm of his sibling around us. Instead of bars between us, now there are little brothers and sisters and friends and parents. We haven't been alone together since our trip down the river. I don't miss prison, but I miss our long talks. I miss the time I could spend just looking at him across the passageway.

Seeing him like this, with a family so large, is difficult to take in. He and his siblings are constantly laughing and talking over one another; it gives me a whole new perspective on this boy I feel so attached to but don't really know. I am happy to see him happy and surrounded by those he loves, but I'm also worried that he might want a family like this of his own. I'm not sure I want to be like Maire and give birth nine times. Plus, I can't help but feel a bit slighted when he spends time with his family instead of just with me. It's a silly feeling and I try to push it away as soon as possible, but it's still there.

One night as I'm reading a book Anna recommended, Maire comes to visit me. Her coldness toward me only lasted a few days. I think I looked too lost and in need of love for such a big-hearted woman to stay distant for long.

"How you gettin' on then, love?" she says.

"It was a good day," I say. As kind as she's been, it isn't like Maire to just show up at my room at night to chat. "Has there been any word on my mother yet?"

Most days I try not to ask about the search for my mother. It is a sore subject, the one topic that strains my relationship with the leadership of the mountain people. Every day that passes with no word makes me feel like I should have been the one to get her out.

"Ah, no, lassie. I'm sorry for that. Joe and I chatted today, and while the boys have checked in with the lookout station by the Institute, they haven't yet contacted your ma."

I look at my empty hands and start to push my cuticles back, wanting to keep my fingers busy. Is Mother just waiting for me at the Institute? Is she being treated well? I feel sick.

"Dear, I need to talk to ya about some other things."

I'm not ready to look her in the eye yet. If she's not here with news about my mother, then it's about Thomas, and I'd rather not be reminded of the fact that I'm the reason her son is rejecting their choice of a wife and going against their customs.

After a minute, I take a deep breath and look up at her. "Oh?"

She pulls the small chair closer to the bed and sits down. I take another breath and face her, hoping to guess from her expression what is coming.

"Dear, I've come to feel quite fond of ya these past couple of weeks, and I can see how ya feel about my Tommy."

*Oh no. This can't be good.*

"But?" I asked.

"But I need ya to understand a few things."

I decide to make it easier for her. "The council made it clear he is promised to someone else. And Adelaide mentioned it even before the meeting."

Maire frowned. "Aye, did she now?"

"Yes. But no one else has said anything since the meeting, not even Thomas. Has something happened?"

"Well, yes and no. You two have been through so much I thought it might be best if we waited a bit before we told you how things are gonna be."

Her phrasing makes me narrow my eyes. "I don't understand."

She sighs and then resolve fills her expression. "Thomas was promised to a girl before he was taken. A very nice girl. She was killed in the raids."

"Oh, no." I can't hold in my gasp, "He never told me."

"He didn't know her well, and he was taken the same time, so I'm not sure if he really ever had time to properly think about marrying her or her dying. You understand?"

"I don't think Thomas is that callous," I say.

"Of course he isn't, but a lot's happened in the last little bit. When we got word from the scouts around the prison that he was alive and in good shape and most likely coming home, well, the committee went ahead and reassigned him another girl, Alice, in good faith."

I shake my head in confusion. "How can you arrange a marriage for someone you haven't even broken out of jail yet?"

"Thomas is a very popular boy. There were yards of girls lined up to be on his list before he was taken, you see. It's not like they've got tons to choose from down here. I mean, there's a fair share, but everyone knows he's most likely going to be a committee head someday, and what girl wouldn't want to be married to him?" She puffs out her chest like a proud mother hen as she explains.

I picture all the brightly dressed girls hugging him when we returned. Was one of them Alice? "Does Alice know?" I ask.

"No, the council hasn't declared the match yet. We were waiting for you young'uns to get your feet back under you."

"Then why was Adelaide talking about Alice?"

Maire's eyes darken. "Adelaide's a busy body, always into everyone's business, listening at doors and such. I should whip her for breathing a word to ya."

"I'm sorry, but if Thomas didn't know and Alice doesn't know, then what's the problem?"

"I'm afraid you are, my dear."

"Why can't you just cancel the engagement and let us be together?" My tone is stronger than I intend, but I'm not backing down.

"That's just the thing." She takes a deep breath before continuing. "The committee is in charge of all that mess, and half of them don't quite trust you yet."

The room isn't as friendly and warm as it was a moment earlier. I feel a squeeze in my chest, like all the times in school when I said something wrong and everyone stared at me as I waited for the instructor to discipline me, call me Neurodeficient, or tell the other children not to be like me.

"What are you saying, Maire?" I am tired of tip-toeing around her point.

"I'm asking you to break with my Tommy." Her face is determined, her jaw set. She's not backing down either.

I should have expected such a request, but the mere idea of separating myself from Thomas is ludicrous. I can't break anything off. I don't want to, and Thomas would never agree. All the years of giving up what I wanted make it easier to stand up for what I want now.

"What if I say no?"

Maire shakes her head in disapproval. "Girl, I knew this wouldn't be easy." She looks at me, her green eyes much older than her face. "Do you know how much pleading I do on your behalf at those meetings? Do you know what I go through for sticking up for you?"

"If they don't like me, why not send me back to Hamen?"

"Because it doesn't work that way. For the love of all that's in this mountain, I wish you'd make this one thing easy on me."

"I'm sorry, Maire, but I just don't understand. It's not like Thomas and I are getting married tomorrow or something—"

"That's exactly it. You ain't serious about each other, but they're afraid you'll lead him off, away from here, and we need him to stay. Aren't many good men left under the mountain. The young'uns get to wondering about what's out there in the big cities, and we never see or hear from them again. It's horrible business, that."

Maire's faces twists like she is going to cry. This ox of a woman who seems to run the whole underground city like she runs her overly large brood of children is breaking down right before my eyes.

I reach out and touch her shoulder. It isn't what my mother would have done, but it's more than I would do when I lived under the constant watch of an autoeye. It feels strange to comfort her, but I do my best.

"I'm so sorry, Maire. I'm sure Thomas has no intention of leaving. He's seen what's outside. I've lived out there. This place is much, much better." I laugh suddenly as the irony hits me hard in the chest. "Maire, I know you've heard me say this, but let me tell you again. All I ever dreamt of when I was a little girl was leaving my community and coming someplace like here. This is my dream."

She sniffs and composes herself quickly. The Maire I know comes back into focus.

"I'm sure that's true, and we all have our dreams, child. I just don't want to see my boy running out on his too soon. Think on what I've said, at least."

She stands to leave and pats me on the shoulder. It feels good to be touched tenderly, but it makes me ache for my mother's arms, for Thomas's arms. I realize as she shuts the door that I long to be held and loved.

# TWELVE

The next day starts early with loud banging on my door. I stumble out of sleep and open the door a crack to see what can be so important. A man I don't recognize stands with arms crossed and face pinched.

"Imani?" he asks.

"Yes."

"You're needed in the council room."

I squint at him. "Is it morning yet?"

"Nearly. Please change quickly. I'll wait for you."

I close the door and turn on my lamp to search for clothing. I can't imagine what they want then realization crashes in—it has to be about Mother. I move as quickly as I can, no longer caring what color clothing I wear or how my hair looks. I throw on my clothes from the day before and tie my hair back in a hasty knot, then take two steps to open the door.

"I'm ready."

The man nods and heads down the hallway toward the main room. I follow, yawning.

Having been underground for so long, I've grown accustomed to the tunnels and darkness. Everything is well lit for the most part, but there are several stretches of lightless tunnel that stand in deep black. After we've walked about ten minutes, the man disappears into one of these patches. It isn't until I approach the next light section of tunnel that I realize he's no longer there.

"Hello?" I call, turning slowly to see where he's gone. My heart beat steadily speeds up.

"This way." His voice comes from the dark behind me.

I squint but can't make him out until he steps closer, gesturing behind him. "The door is here."

I walk back into the dark, putting my hands out carefully in front of me. Sure enough, the wall ends and another tunnel branches off the main one—a tunnel I'd never noticed before.

As we plunge into the inky black, my mind becomes more clear, my nerves more alert. Everything is new and strange and I start to feel my muscles flexing involuntarily. I'm ready to run or fight if I need to. There aren't any lights here, and I stumble a few times on the rough floor, catching myself on the tunnel wall. Should I even be following this man? I am considering turning back when he announces, "We're here."

Ahead of us in the tunnel, I can make out the glowing outline of a door. He reaches it first, grabs a handle, and pulls, filling the shaft with light. I cover my eyes and take a few careful steps forward.

Once my vision adjusts, I see a large dark brown wooden

table filling most of the room and ten to fifteen people seated in metal chairs around it. I recognize Joe and Minerva, and I think one other is the outspoken Ernest from my first interview with the council, but the others are strangers, men and women I may have seen once or twice but have never spoken to. Joe sits at the head of the table, Minerva on his right. Though hewn from stone, like the passage, it is warm and filled with a golden light coming from three hanging pendant lights. The air is dense with so many bodies in the space and no ventilation, but I'm glad it's warm at least.

"Where are Maire and Thomas?" I ask the man who's led me here.

"They were not invited." He turns from my side and sits in the chair to Joe's left.

"Their presence is not necessary for this meeting," Minerva says. She sounds just like one of the Leaders, sure of herself, the laws, and her place at the table—pure authority. I look around, unsure of whether to sit or flee.

Joe clears his throat. "Imani, please have a seat." He motions to a chair opposite him at the other end of the table. I pull it out and sit on the edge, feeling anxious. "We have come together this morning to talk about a few issues."

"My mother?" I can't hold it in any longer. All I need is a yes or a no.

"Excuse me?" Joe cocks his head in confusion.

I frown. He can't possibly have forgotten. "Have you had

any news from your men about my mother?" I press.

"Ah, yes." He nods his head in understanding, then continues, "That is to say, no, we haven't had word yet. The boys are still down mountain looking for signs of her." He turns to address the group. "As I was saying, we must discuss a few items as a council. I have invited Miss Imani here today as I feel she may be a valuable asset to us as we move forward with whatever direction we take.

"The flat lands are becoming increasingly restless. I have word that the Secondary School rebellion has escalated. They have taken control of several supply trains and nearby production communities. This could mean a shortage of food for our people as well as others throughout our land."

Guilt washes over me. I have been so wrapped up in Thomas, teaching, and finding my mother that I let the problems I'd started at school slip from my mind. It feels like another life. I steady my breathing and try to focus on what Joe is saying.

"Gary tells me we have roughly nineteen months' worth of food, strictly rationed, in our food storage and gardens, but that depends on the harvest next fall. We must decide which of these parties to align with to keep our people safe and fed."

"This sounds like as good a time as any to split from the Leaders," an old man seated near the center of the table proclaims.

Joe nods. "I understand your position, Hector. My concern is who or what takes the Leaders' place if they are defeated."

"At least with the Leaders in charge, we always know when our next meal is coming," a middle-aged woman with black hair adds.

Hector scoffs. "Or our next raid. They aren't worth trusting or helping."

"Before we begin debate, we need more information about the strengths of the Leaders. They appear weak, but we've never been able to discover their weaponry stores." He turns to me. "In the past, we sent reconnaissance teams to verify rumors and help us plot our moves, but we lose a lot of good men that way, and I'm fairly certain that we won't need them this time."

"You got a magic wand up your sleeve, Joe?" Hector laughs, and a few around the table join in.

"Magic is not *of use*," Minerva says, and laughter rolls around the room.

"Actually, I do," Joe says and looks in my direction.

"Me?" I place my hand on my chest.

Joe nods. "You told us that Hamen put information into your mind instead of wiping it. Now it's time to put that information to use."

Beads of sweat break out on my forehead as they all look at me, the laughter sucked from the room. I am cornered in my cell at the prison again. I never should have told them what Hamen did.

"Imani?"

"Yes?"

"Will you agree to help us?"

"I'm not sure I can." I've been trying to avoid thinking about the information crammed in my brain as a form of self-preservation—the less I think about it, the less painful memory episodes I have. Letting them get a glimpse of just how much I know, and about what, could be very dangerous. I decide to try to play dumb and bluff until I can get out of the room and talk to Thomas. We can figure out what to do.

"You're not sure you can, or you're not sure you will?" Minerva says.

"I literally don't know what happened. One minute I was in the prison yard, the next I was waking up in a Mind Wipe chamber after being shot. Hamen was ranting over me and then my mind was filled with all sorts of information. It was so painful I passed out again. I woke up in the institute. That's it."

Joe looks at her and then down at his hands. "Let me fill in a few of the gaps, Imani." He nods, and the man who led me to the meeting stands up and takes a wide leg stance in front of the door. I grip the sides of my chair and squeeze. The room is growing smaller.

"After our chat in the common room a few weeks ago, I started gathering more information on Hamen and the Blue Spider Alliance. It seems you were correct about his experimenting on subjects. For quite some time, at least a decade, he has been erasing their memories and records of their past lives as the Mind Wipe program required, but then he fills their heads with information from the past."

Panic creeps into my gut. How did Joe find all this out?

"Imani, you said he filled you with *all the information.* What exactly did you mean by that?"

I can see the lab clearly in my mind—the machines, Hamen standing over me talking about his good intentions, his plans. Instruments in his hands. The raging pain in my head as he turned on the machine and images flashed in my mind, faster, faster, faster.

"Imani?" he asks, more gently now.

"Sorry," I apologize, still unsure of what to say. What do they want from me?

"We aren't going to hurt you. I imagine that between Secondary School and prison, you aren't quite sure who to trust."

There's that word again—trust.

"I'm guessing he used you as a test subject and implanted information without first wiping your mind?"

All I can do is nod while the whole room stares in silence.

"We would like you to allow us access to that information," Joe says, as if he's asking to borrow my ration cards or a school reader.

"How?" I ask. There is no way I am letting anyone hook me up to any of those machines again.

"There won't be any sort of extraction technique like Hamen uses. We were hoping you might be able to just tell us what we need to know."

I'm already shaking my head. "It's not that simple. It's not like I have a mental encyclopedia with an index to easily search the information. I don't understand the information he put in me, though most of it seems related to art and music—you know, cultural things. I can't control it, and it takes over my brain at unexpected times, often painfully. The episodes exhaust and confuse me. I've spent the days since waking up trying to push them back..." My voice trails off as watch Joe exchange a glance with Minerva.

Minerva leans toward me, looking deep in my eyes as if searching for the answers she wants. "We need to know if you know anything that can stop this Secondary School rebellion. We need your promise that you'll do all you can to bring any useful memories to the surface for us."

I find it ironic that I'm currently *of use* to them. "I don't know how to do that," I respond honestly.

"When the thoughts came in the past, what prompted them to appear?" Joe asks.

"Usually something someone says triggers a related entry, but it doesn't always—"

"So if I said the Institute?"

I frown, frustrated at his interruption. "No, you don't understand. Saying random words doesn't mean the memories will be triggered. I don't know why they surface sometimes and not others, and some of the images are terrifying—death, war, murder... I've been working hard to make it all go away."

"Imani." Minerva stands. "You must learn to recall those memories. We want to know everything Hamen has stuffed in your head about the Institute, the government, the Leaders, and anything else useful. You will be given a reader for recording your discoveries. Please notify us if you discover anything useful." She looks down her nose at me. "After all the trouble you've caused at the Secondary School, this is the least you can do."

I had been thinking of ways to avoid reporting to them, but her words are like a blow and I cringe away from her. I know she's right.

"Sit down, Minerva," Joe says calmly. "Imani, we intend to move out of the mountain, back into the sunlight, but we can't do that unless we conquer those who want to keep us locked in the earth or subjected to their will. Can you please try to access anything you might know about the government, their plans, and Hamen? The information in your head could save thousands of lives."

His sincerity pierces me and I nod. "Yes. I will try." It really is the least I can do to after leaving my friends to deal with my mess at the Secondary School. Minerva's nod of satisfaction makes me wary, though. She is the kind of woman I can easily picture hurting someone for the fun of it. She doesn't seem like the other mountain folk. I wonder if she came from the flat lands.

"Then I guess we'll *try* look for your mother," Minerva

says, mocking my hesitation.

I look at her, shocked. "What do you mean?"

"You want to see your mother again, correct?" she says.

"Of course. You already promised you'd go after her." I look at Joe questioningly.

Joe shifts in his seat uncomfortably.

Minerva sniffs. "And that is no little favor you asked of us. Consider your reports a token of appreciation for our efforts. What we are asking of you is merely a mental exercise. We need maps, diagrams, secret entrances, histories, weaknesses— everything."

"Minerva, such intimidation is not necessary. I'm sure Imani will tell us anything she can," Joe says calmly.

"I'm sure Imani doesn't know what it's like to slowly starve to death, or watch her loved ones die at the hands of the Leaders," Minerva shoots back.

Her venom triggers something ugly in me that's been sleeping. The starved body of 345 flashes across my eyes—my own painful memory instead of an inserted one.

I stand up fast enough to knock my chair back. It hits the stone floor with a clang. "You have no idea what I have and haven't been through. I don't pretend to know what's happened to turn you into such a cold, dispassionate woman. Give me the reader and something to write with and we'll see what comes up, but don't think for a minute that anything useful is the consequence of your threats and abuse of authority. I'm volunteering to dig through information that has been surgically implanted in my brain against my will in order to help my friends who are suffering at the hands of the Leaders and for the young ones here who deserve to live above ground."

Someone huffs at my insolence and Minerva stares for a beat before she pulls a paper reader from a stack next to her on the table and slides me the pencil she's kept behind her ear since the meeting began.

I walk towards the door, praying the man will step aside and let me go without a fight.

He doesn't. I pause, not willing to turn around and ask for permission to be released.

"Imani," Joe says.

I look over my shoulder at him.

"Just do the best you can. We are all on the same side. I'll let you know when I hear about your mother."

I nod and turn back toward the door. The man steps aside and opens it for me. I slip into the tunnel beyond and the door closes with a *clap,* leaving me in darkness. I hesitate for a moment, adjusting to the lack of light and fiddling with the paper in my hands. I hear the drone of voices pick up beyond the door. Curious, I step closer and press my ear to the thick wood.

"—if she finds out?" a man's nasally voice is asking.

"She's not going to find out. Besides, as long as we get what we need, it won't matter," Minerva says, her clipped voice cutting through the door easily.

Joe responds, his quiet deep voice harder to make out. "It does matter... I'll deal with... if and when it happens. Now, how... deal with this water pump... Can we get the part... community 486?"

I step backward, trying not to make any noise on the uneven stone floor. They are not telling me everything, just like Hamen didn't tell me everything. Of course, I don't know for certain who the "she" is they are talking about hiding things from, but it seems likely to be me. I need to talk to Maire and Thomas about the meeting as soon as I see them again.

Speaking of, why weren't they at the meeting? Maire seems to hold quite a bit of clout with the community. When I am with her, people ask for her support and opinion on matters big and small.

I continue puzzling as I walk to the main hall for breakfast. I bump into Thomas just outside the turn to my room.

His face brightens in delight. "There's my lovely girl!"

"Good morning," I say, a smile spreading across my face despite my concerns.

He looks up and down the deserted passageways then grins at me like a wolf. "Would you look there? We are all by ourselves."

He reaches out. I hesitate, then sink into his arms. They feel so safe, and I close my eyes and sigh in relief. I startle when his lips press against mine, but it feels good. I breathe deeply and force myself to relax, to take in the moment and to enjoy just being together like I've been wanting for these past weeks. I kiss him back, slowly and with my eyes closed this time. After a moment he leans back, his quick smile spreading warmth through my whole body.

"I won't be needing much breakfast now. Nothing as sweet as you down there in the ovens."

"You might not be needing much of anything," I say, "but I'm starving. Let's go eat." I have been trying to pick up more of the local vernacular, but it is difficult.

Thomas laughs at my efforts then pulls me in for another kiss.

"Eh-hem." We jump apart as a passing miner clears his throat. Thomas waves merrily at him as I blush and giggle. Once he's gone, Thomas leans over and whispers, "We need to get out of here." His lips brush the sensitive skin of my ear, sending tingles up and down my spine. "I need to see you alone for once, and I need some sunshine. What do you say? Fancy skipping school today?"

I haven't had a chance to tell him about Maire's visit last night. I'm not sure if I will. I don't like to think of him resenting his mother for trying to separate us, and I'm not letting him go. It is no secret that we are together, and I'm open about my plans to stay with the mountain community. This is the life I dreamed of—I am free to go where I want, do what I want, be who I want to be, to an extent—and I have Thomas.

I stand on tip toes and brush my mouth across his ear, hoping to cause the same sensations for him. "I say yes."

"Aren't you the devil in a blue dress?" He laughs and takes my hand. "We're going to need food for where we're going, and warm clothes."

My heart skips a beat. Good food, Thomas, and adventure are exactly what I need to wash away the uncomfortable morning.

As we enter the dining hall, a little boy from one of my classes rushes up to me, taking my hand.

"Are you coming to talk to us again today?" he asks.

"Not today. But I'll be there tomorrow. What would like to learn about?" I say.

"I want to hear more about the dead animals. The ones that used to be here but aren't now. Like the dinosaurs and horses."

"We'll have an animal day for your class tomorrow," I say.

He smiles and runs off to rejoin his family for breakfast. Adelaide is sitting at a table next to his, staring at me. I shake off her cold eyes and turn away.

I notice two men sitting at the end of a table closer to us, bent over bowls of steaming oatmeal. One has a nasty scar on his cheek. They are talking in low grunts and keeping to themselves. They wear the uniforms of guards and have rifles propped against the table. Something about them strikes me as familiar, but I can't quite place them.

Thomas gives my hand another squeeze then drops it to pick up bowls for both of us. I tuck my reader and pencil under my arm and take a bowl. The food smells amazing. Thomas stuffs a small bag full of bread and apples and fills our bowls with oatmeal, then smiles at me like I am the only girl in the world.

It is going to be an amazing day.

# THIRTEEN

Thomas takes my hand to lead me down a new set of tunnels that I have somehow missed in the past few weeks. We duck into a supply room and forage for winter coats and boots. He hands me a red hat.

"That ought to look nice on ya." He smiles.

I twist my hair up on top of my head and pull the hat over it. "Do I look like a real mountain girl now?"

"Yes, but you'll always be a flatlander to me."

I move to punch him in the arm, but he dances away, grinning, before leading me back into the tunnel to join a throng of miners heading to their daily tasks. Soon we split off the main tunnel and start up a long stairway. Thomas holds my hand tightly in his as we bounce up the worn, stacked stones, laughing and whispering. My heart beats like a bird flapping its wings in a cage.

I used to skip chores and classes regularly, but never with someone else. I was always alone when I hiked up the hill behind my pod to lay in the spring grass and stare at the clouds drifting above me. I didn't mind being alone, but being alone with Thomas, a boy I like, is an entirely new feeling—entirely wonderful.

Eventually we come to a passage with walls of stacked square stones. A cool breeze catches my coat and blows it back, forcing me to pause and zip up the front.

"Not much farther. How does that fresh air feel to you?"

"Fantastic!" I take a huge breath and let it fill my body with tingles. I smell snow and pine and crispness. I didn't realize how accustomed to the smell of dust and mildew I had become.

After a few minutes walking, the tunnel begins to grow gradually lighter, and we approach an ancient wooden door with a rusted metal latch. Thomas smiles at me in the dim light, takes my hand, then leans into the door and shoves his whole weight into the latch with his shoulder, forcing it up and out.

Sunlight kisses our faces, blinding us for a moment.

"Whoa! Now there's a spark of sun for you," Thomas says as he holds up his free hand to shield the light while his eyes adjust. I follow suit, blinking as the trees begin to take shape around me.

Thomas pushes the door closed behind us. "Come on, let's get our giddy up going."

I follow through the ankle-deep snow. "Where are we going?"

"The old homes. Not all of us were cave dwellers." He points through the trees and stomps forward, breaking a snow trail for me.

A few minutes later, we come to a strip cleared of trees and covered in a thick blanket of snow pocked with a few sets of animal tracks. We tromp along the old road in silence for a few more minutes until the still mountain air is filled with the trilling song of a bird.

"Oh!" I say and stop walking to search the trees for the source of the song.

The singing abruptly stops as well and Thomas's laugh fills the air instead.

"What kind of bird was that? Did you see it?" I ask.

He laughs even harder. "Aye, sweets."

"What?"

He puts both hands on my hips and pulls me in, puckering his lips like a fish, not exactly inviting a kiss. The song bursts from his mouth and fills the woods once more.

"How are you doing that?" I ask, amazed.

He smiles and pulls me closer. "It's called whistling, and every child big enough for their boots learns to do it to help pass the time while he's working."

"But how?"

He shows me how to purse my lips and blow with just the right pressure to make a sweet note trip into the air. I try my best, but other than air, all that comes out are little spit droplets.

"Stop. Just stop it, lass." He laughs again and puts a hand to my lips before leaning in for a real kiss. No fish lips involved.

*Human whistling is the production of sound by means of carefully controlling a stream of air flowing through a small hole. Whistling can be achieved by creating a small opening with one's lips and then blowing or sucking air through the hole. The air is moderated by the lips, tongue, teeth, or fingers (placed over the mouth) to create turbulence, and the mouth acts as a resonant chamber to enhance the resulting sound by acting as a type of Helmholtz resonator.*

I pull back and rub at my temples. The pain is sharp and quick. But out in the open forest with just Thomas to focus on, I let my defenses down and relax for the first time in months, opening a gate that will likely flood me with information.

"What is it?" Thomas looks genuinely concerned.

"Nothing, just a headache. It will pass. Just give me a minute."

"You get those a lot."

"Only when the information pops up."

"You mean the stuff Hamen jammed in your head?" His eyebrows draw down into a scowl.

"Yes." I take a deep breath. I have so much to tell him, especially about the meeting this morning. But not yet. I don't want anything about this day to be darkened by our past or by Hamen. "Let's keep walking, and you keep whistling. I promise to be quiet."

"Alrighty then." He takes my hand and leads me down the

road, deeper into the woods.

A group of buildings slowly becomes visible through the trees. They are nothing like the sleek white pods I grew up in. The rough, brown dwellings are made of logs stacked on top of one another, and peaked grass-covered rooftops are visible in areas where the snow has already melted.

"Is this where you used to live?"

I take in the small buildings and other signs that life once flourished here, stacks of wood between trees, steps to a house that no longer stands, carts rusting and forgotten. All of it is abandoned now, snow piled up against the doors or blown into homes left open. Toward the edge of the grouping, a few buildings have been reduced to half-charred walls poking out of the white snow.

A few footprints, half filled with snow, mar the snow. Some are from humans, some from animals. My mind starts to hum and vibrate with definitions and identifications as I stare at the indentations in the snow. I immediately focus on something else and push the information back with another deep breath.

Thomas stops swinging our arms so vigorously and slows. We've reached an open space in the center of the buildings. His face is sober—not so much sad as contemplative. I haven't seen him serious like this since the first council meeting I was a part of.

"This is the center of town or used to be. After they raided us, everyone left for the mines. Some folks already lived down there, and we always kept provisions for emergencies anyway, so there was no reason to come back here. They took all the bodies with them, dead or alive. My family had a place up that way." Thomas points past the burned homes. "What I wanted to show you is right here though."

He hikes confidently toward one of the larger buildings and pulls the door open, scraping the snow back in an arc. Inside it is dark and musty smelling. Long, low counters filled with household items stand in front of towering shelves holding even more items, including tools, fabrics, and long-term shelf foods.

"What is this place?" I've never seen anything like it. How could one person or family be allowed to have so much?

"We called it the general store. It's where we got all the things we needed for day-to-day living."

I nod slowly, considering. "We had everything delivered to us according to our allowance."

"Delivered? How did they know what you needed?"

"I don't know. I suppose they kept logs for food and clothing. If we ever needed something extra, we applied for it and, depending on our needs, it would either be accepted or rejected."

"By who?"

"The Leaders."

Thomas shakes his head and steps behind a counter. I run my finger along the top, digging a path through the dust.

"How long have you been living in the mine?"

Thomas rummages around under the shelves. "About nine months or so now. Though I'm not sure how long I was in prison, exactly." He sticks his head up and smiles at me. "Never been much for dates." He dives back under the counter, shuffling and scraping sounds resuming. He pops up after a minute, holding a piece of woodwork in his hands.

"What is that?"

Before Thomas can answer, a flood of information overpowers me. Sounds, images, and definitions fill my mind, riding on a wave of pain. I try to relax and let it flow.

*The violin, also known as a fiddle, is a string instrument, usually with four strings tuned in perfect fifths. It is the smallest, highest-pitched member of the violin family of string instruments, which also includes the viola, the cello, and the double bass.*

Thomas is around the corner in a flash, his arms around me as I hold my head and moan. "Breathe a bit there, lass."

I take a deep breath of dusty air and push hard at the images in my mind until nothing is left but a single melody. It is beautiful, haunting, and helps me relax. I stand up straight and blink, the pain lingering.

"I'm sorry," I say, angry and embarrassed. I hate that I can be overcome by artificial memories at any moment, especially when I should be relaxed and enjoying my day with Thomas.

I force myself to focus on the music, and the pain subsides. I look at him. "I'm so sorry."

"You don't have to apologize for anything, love. That was a bad one, eh?" Thomas studies me with concern.

"Yeah. But I'm starting to get a hold on it." I don't want him to worry, so I continue, "Show me the violin. Do you know how to play it?" The sweet melody still trills in my mind, slowly fading as I walk toward the counter where Thomas set the violin before checking on me.

"Ah, not really. I've messed around a bit with it. I can pick out a melody or two." He plucks the instrument carefully from the dusty surface and turns the pegs at one end, testing the tone of the strings.

"Where did you get it? I thought these were all destroyed during the wars." The wood is rough and the finish dull. It is obviously not the instrument of a great master.

"I made it." He looks down and blushes.

My eyes widen in wonder. "That's amazing, Thomas."

"Well, don't get excited just yet." He lifts the instrument to his shoulder and begins to pluck the strings in a sweet little tune sprinkled with sour notes. The sound is nothing like the music in my mind, but watching him so intently plucking at the strings and sliding his fingers around trying to find the right positions is so endearing, I can't help but prefer it.

After a few minutes, he stops and I clap enthusiastically.

"Needs a bit of work, but yah. That's what I wanted to show

you." He gives me a self-conscious grin and fiddles nervously with the pegs. "They used to use horse hair to make the bows— you know, the stick you pull across the strings? But I couldn't tell you where any horses are these days, so I figured some music is better than no music, right?"

"It's absolutely wonderful! Can I hold it?"

"Of course." He steps closer and hands it to me. "You've got to hold her like this."

His warm hands brush mine and our shoulders rub together as he places the handmade violin on my shoulder. I pluck carefully at the wire used for strings and giggle at my own abysmal attempt to play.

I examine it, praising his hard work and asking him questions. We take turns passing it back and forth as he explains how he made certain parts and I re-inspect it.

"It's good to have it out and playing again," he says.

"Why did you leave it here? Weren't you afraid someone would take it?"

"No. No one comes up here anymore. And after the raids there aren't many that's fond of making music. It reminds them of the folks who were killed or taken that day. I stashed it back here before they nabbed me." He moves behind the counter to put it away. I long to hold it again and take it with me, but I understand his need for discretion.

"So what are we going to do now?" I ask, hoping for more surprises.

"I dunno," he says as he stands up from behind the counter, a wicked smile on his face. "I have a couple of ideas, but it's up to you."

He reaches out and pulls me around the corner to meet him face to face among the shelves of abandoned cans and trinkets. I look up into his smiling eyes before I close my own and kiss him, letting the bubbly feelings flow from my mouth to my heart and stomach, finally resting in my hands and feet.

I am absolutely warm, safe, and complete in his arms, sharing his breath and feeling his heart beat in time with mine. But eventually I have to pull back to catch my breath.

"What's the matter?" He smiles down at me.

"I just can't breathe." I laugh and feel my body longing to be closer to his.

"You're going to have to work on that a bit, lassie."

"Work on what?" I tense with self-consciousness.

"Breathing," he says. "It might take lots and lots of practice."

He suddenly bends and lifts me off the ground. I squeal with surprise at the quick movement and the ease with which he carries me.

"Where are you taking me?"

"Does it matter?"

"Yes." I pound his shoulder playfully.

"Hold your breath, I'm going to kiss you again."

We both laugh as he kisses me then pushes through a door

into what appears to be a living space for whomever ran the shop before it was abandoned. The walls are hung with colored fabrics and paintings. The furniture is handmade from rough-hewn wood and of all different configurations, covered in soft pillows of bright colors. The kitchen is full of the same things that cover the shelves in the store—strange metal contraptions, wooden bowls, cans of food, sacks of beans and flour. I've never seen so much food left out in the open. The space is so different from my home and even from the mines.

Thomas kisses me again and pushes through another door to a sleeping area where a large bed covered in a multi-colored quilt sits against one wall. He drops me unceremoniously on one side and collapses on top of me. I laugh and wiggle to get out from under him, but he kisses me again and I pull him closer and let myself float in the moment. The early morning council meeting, Minerva and Joe, Maire's request, Adelaide's dislike of me, even the unsuccessful search for my mother—all fade into unimportance as I finally have Thomas and his smiles to myself.

We stay that way for what feels like hours—kissing, laughing, teasing each other. When we get cold, we snuggle under the colorful quilt, and for lunch Thomas pulls apples and rolls from the pockets of his coat for us to snack on. Only when the sun's evening rays pour through the window do we fall apart, exhausted and sighing.

"I'm starving." I smooth flyaway hairs away from my face, and the cool air washes over my exposed arms like a cold shower heightening my senses and sharpening my appetite. Our coats, boots, and hats are in a pile by the door, ditched long ago to get closer to one another.

"Speak no more." Thomas jumps from the bed and bows deeply. "I'll fetch your afternoon meal in a jiffy hop, lass."

"A jiffy hop?" I laugh.

"Of course, nothing faster. Quick as a whip." He bounds out the door we came in. I sit up on the bed and lean back against the wall, examining the beautiful quilt made of all different colors of scraps sewn together with tiny stitches. Curtains sewn in the same style hang from the walls covering the windows, but the one across from me is parted just enough that I can see the snow and trees outside, golden in the light of the setting sun.

Thomas's warmth is starting to leave me, so I pull the quilt up to my shoulders, wrapping my arms around myself. I smile as I think about him. I can't remember another time in my life when I've been this completely happy. This must have been what it was like back when people were allowed to choose their spouses based on love and physical attraction. My parents, chosen for each other by the Leaders, were happy together, or at least I thought they were. Thomas's society is much more relaxed than mine was, but the marriages are still arranged by the community leaders. There's no room to meet someone, accidentally fall in love, and find your way together. This is the first time I've thought about my own marriage or eventual family. Immediate survival always seemed more important. Sitting in this colorful bed in this cold little house, waiting for him to return, I can almost see myself building my own family for the first time.

I hear his soft footfalls on the wood floor coming closer to entering the bedroom. I snuggle down in giddy anticipation, but a shadow moves along the far wall, catching my eye—someone is passing the window on the opposite side of the room.

The shot of adrenaline that pulses through my body makes Thomas's footfalls and my breaths sound thunderous. I sink down into the quilt and freeze, hoping the bedding will swallow me whole as I stare at the small strip of glass visible between the curtains. At the same time Thomas steps into the room, a face appears in the window—its eyes just as wide and shocked as mine when we see each other.

Thomas throws a bag on the bed then pounces on me, kissing my neck. I tense, craning to look around him.

He pulls back in confusion. "What is it, love?"

I point. "Someone's at the window."

# FOURTEEN

Thomas rolls over and his gaze follows my finger to the slip of glass. The face has vanished into the snowy day. "Who was it?" He slides to the edge of the bed and puts his boots and coat back on.

My glimpse of the face had been quick, but I recognized the brown eyes. "I think it was Adelaide."

"What the blazes is she doing out here?" Thomas jumps to his feet and heads for the door.

"Where are you going?" I follow after him, slinging my coat over my shoulders and stuffing my feet into the now cold boots, then replacing the red hat on my head. I take a moment to tuck my hair back up while he answers.

"To fetch that little whellep and give her a talking to, that's where."

He is already out the front door by the time I reach the store and get my coat fastened again. I can hear him calling her, followed by her reply. I hesitate for a moment. Do I really want to get in the middle of this?

Yes. I have to know what is going on.

"You are a traitor! I'm turning you into the council, Thomas. You bloody, lying eegit!"

"What are you talking about? I haven't lied or done anything wrong, Adelaide," Thomas says, his voice steady and calm.

"Then what are you doing out here with *her*?" I round the corner and meet Adelaide's gaze when she lifts a finger at me.

"That is none of your bloody business. I might ask the same of you. What are you doing out here?" Thomas says.

"I'm checking up on my big brother and his no-good plans. What do you suppose is going on down there while you're up here sucking face with this flatlander?"

"Adelaide—"

"They're making plans to raid the Leaders and you're missing out on all of it because you've been mooning around after her." She points at me again and scowls. "Plus, everyone is all up in a dither wondering what your intentions are toward Alice."

"I think you're the one in a dither. I've already told them I don't have any intentions toward her, Adelaide. I never have."

"Fantastic. And how about toward *us*? You got any intentions for your family anymore? Your home?"

Thomas runs his hand through his hair and looks down at the ground, kicking a lump of snow with his boot. "Everything changed in prison." He speaks so softly, it's as if his thoughts escaped accidentally.

"Nothing changed here." Adelaide raises her voice, her face

hard, her hands clenched.

"Plenty changed here." He looks her in the eye now. "Since when do we go around attacking the Leaders? We've done just fine up here avoiding them since the raid. Who's crazy-brained idea is it to head out of our hidey hole into their fires?"

"That's *exactly* why we need you, Thomas. You think more clearly than anyone else, and you've seen the outside—you know what they can do to us. You were born to lead us. Don't forget that."

"Oh, criminy, Adel. That's a bunch of poppy-cocksy and you know it." Thomas folds his arms, taking a determined stance in the snow.

"You and your poppy-cocksy are what's going to get us in trouble, following this she-beast around everywhere. She's going to lead you right back into their hands."

As I hear her description of me, something snaps, and I step forward, thrusting my own finger toward Adelaide to punctuate my words. "I'm sick and tired of other people assuming they know me, what I want, and what I'm going to do. I have no desire to return to the flat lands. The Leaders ruined my life. Why would I ever go back to that when I've spent my whole life trying to get away?"

Adelaide rolls her eyes, unmoved by my speech. "Sure they did. So now you prance your pretty face and your longy-lash hair up here to our home to ruin it for us."

"I don't know who you think you are," I take a step closer,

my voice soft, "but I've dealt with Leaders, prison guards, psychotic old ladies, and evil professors. If I have to make *whiny little sisters* next on my list, I'm happy to."

This time my words seems to rattle her a bit, and she looks away. Younger than me, but taller, she has arms thick with a lifetime of heavy labor in the mines before her classroom assignment. She is probably twice as strong as me, but something tells me her bark is much worse than her bite. She is worried about Thomas and is most likely just scared and confused—like the rest of us.

"If you two would spend five seconds getting to know each other, I swear you'd be best mates in a flash." Thomas is actually laughing.

Now it's my turn to scowl at him.

"I know you both better than you know yourselves. You should trust me on this one."

"How do you know her at all? You've only just met her." Adelaide tosses her head in my direction.

"I know her just fine, Adel. She's a good person and I trust her. So should you."

"Whatever. I don't even trust you right now, Thomas, much less the likes of her."

"What would you have me do then? Hmm?" Thomas says.

"Get your arse back down the mountain and do what you were born to do!" She stomps her foot like a little one and balls up her fists.

Thomas lets out an audible groan and runs his hand through his thick hair again. I did the same thing earlier that day, combing my fingers through the soft strands. I suddenly feel overwhelmed by the urge to hold him, to comfort him. I take the few steps needed to close the gap between us and I put my arm around his waist. He immediately wraps his arms around me.

"Ugh!" Adelaide throws her hands up in the air and turns away from us, stomping through the snow. "You two make me sick."

As I watch her walk through the white woods, her feet crunching with each step, I ask, "Do you need to go after her?"

"Naw. I'll give her some time to cool down first."

"What does she mean, do what you're born to do?"

"Ah. It's nothing. Just some gobbledy gook about our family and me being the eldest and all."

"And?" There's more to it—I can tell by how he doesn't meet my eyes.

He kisses my forehead then looks at me straight on. "Joe Finnis is my uncle, but he's got no kids, so I'm supposed to take over once he's done leading. But that ain't going to be for a long, long time. Joe's got the fire of life burning in him brighter than the noonday sun. He'll be around for a lot of years yet."

"Do you want to take over?" I ask.

"You know," he smiles, "you're the first person to ever ask me that. And that's why I love you, Miss Imani."

He leans in and kisses me softly. I kiss him back, but the

phrase gives me pause. Love isn't *of use*. I've been told that my whole life. But knowing he loves me, that my mother loved me, I also realize I love them both. And love seems like something that could be very useful if I could have it every day without boundaries and hiding.

I pull back after a minute. "What about Alice?"

Thomas groans again.

"Well?" I ask. "I told your mother we weren't madly in love."

"Are we though?" he asks, a grin dancing on his lips. He knows what I will say.

"I think so."

"Good," he says. "Then I need to talk to her."

"I think you do too." I give him my most serious look.

"I'll do it tonight. Crikey. Look at what a mess you've made of my life!"

If he hadn't laughed as he said this, and pulled me closer for another kiss, I might have burst into tears and run away. Instead, I take the joke as it is meant and enjoy the warm embrace in the cold air.

When my stomach growls mid-kiss, we pull apart laughing and return to the store where Thomas picks up the bag of food he left on the bed. We take our time eating and laughing. I ask him questions about the peculiar items on the walls and shelves of the store, but more often than not, I know more than he does once my implanted memories kicked in. I am getting better at controlling them, calling them forward as I need, and keeping them back when not. It's still hard to remember to relax when I start to feel the tingle of information surging, but when I do, it doesn't hurt as much.

There is still an uneasiness in the air from his sister's visit. I can't shake the feeling that someone else is watching us—a feeling I'd left behind in prison.

"Where to now?" I ask once we've exhausted the items in the store.

"How's about uptown to my old place?" He offers me his hand and slings the knapsack over his shoulder.

"Sounds great."

But as he starts to open the door, he closes it just as quickly again.

"What's wrong?" I whisper.

"There's two biggies out there."

"Biggies?"

"Yah. Big guards."

"Leaders?" My heart starts to pound at the thought of being hauled back to jail.

"No, they're from down the mount, my people, but it still wouldn't do to be caught up here without permission."

"Aren't they going to see our tracks anyway?"

"Yah." He pulls me toward the back of the store again. "We'd better go out the window."

I slide my way along the wall so I can peer out, hopefully

unnoticed. I wanted to see these *biggies* for myself.

It is the same two men I'd seen in the dining hall—same uniforms, same guns on their backs. They are talking to themselves as they walk with silent steps up the old road, passing right next to the store. I am able to watch them more closely now than back in the mines. As I study their faces, I see the one with a thick scar on his cheek and suddenly remember where I know them from: they were the men sent to rescue my mother.

"**T**homas, look," I say.

Thomas takes my place at the window and peers out the part in the curtains.

"Those are the men Joe sent to get my mother from Hamen." I can't believe I didn't make the connection that morning.

He studies them longer than I think necessary before saying, "You're right."

"We have to go. We have to ask them what happened, if they found her, how—where she is!"

I reach for the door but Thomas puts his hand on my shoulder.

"We can't right now, Imani. We're not supposed to be up here without permission, and we're sure shooting not supposed to be up here alone together."

I take a deep breath. Information about my mother seems more important than any consequence for being up here without permission, but Thomas knows his people better than I do. Maybe the men wouldn't tell us anything about my mother and we'd still get in trouble. I have to trust Thomas.

"Then we need to get back to the mine. What are they doing up here anyway? I saw them this morning at breakfast but didn't recognize them right off. Wouldn't they be in meetings or something? Resting? What do you think happened? They would have told me if they brought her back, right?"

"Slow down, missy." Thomas takes my hand gently in his. "We best get out the back before they come hunting us."

Reluctant, I follow him to the back of the house where he pries open the window his sister had been spying in and starts to climb out.

"What if she's there, Thomas? What if they found her and brought her back? Maybe they are looking for me right now and I am running around outside. We've got to hurry." I can't slow my mind down. A myriad of possibilities fly through my thoughts as I follow him.

"Lassie, you've got to keep your voice down. Just don't say anything until we're back in the tunnel. Got it?" he whispers.

I nod and creep behind him through the snow, retracing his sister's footprints. Even with the temptation of knowing more about my mother, and possibly seeing her, I am still a little disappointed that my day with Thomas was cut short. He keeps a firm hold on my hand. It feels good but not good enough to calm my nerves.

We make it through the woods without seeing the guards again, or anyone else. The heavy door is half hidden by a tree, and the snow helps to make the entrance look like just another large rock on the mountain side. Multiple sets of footprints are left from people coming and going from the opening; it seems we aren't the only ones sneaking out today.

Thomas heaves on the handle and pulls it back far enough for me to enter first. I blink several times, trying to acclimate to the darkness inside. As Thomas shuts the door behind us, I take another deep breath, and we plunge into the passage.

"Where is Joe right now?" I ask.

"Prolly cutting down in the ore tunnel. But don't get any ideas—you can't head down there willy nilly to ask him a question. You don't have clearance or a helmet. I'll get my gear and go talk to him. You'll want to wait for me in the classroom."

"I can't just go back to the classroom and help out while you are talking about my mother. What if she's here? What if he's not in the tunnel because he's helping with her, getting her settled in, or talking to her about Hamen?"

"Alrighty, that's fine. Just pick a place where you can wait, and I'll track him down. It's the fastest way for me to find out what's what."

"The common room. I'll meet you there."

"Hungry?" There is a smile in his voice.

"No. My stomach is all in knots. I just want to know what happened to Mother."

We are flying down the steps in the dark, and soon I begin to see a light ahead.

"That's the main tunnel. Take it to the left and you'll be able to find your way after that. It might take me the better part of an hour, alrighty? So don't go running off. I'll come back."

"I'll wait."

Light spills over his shoulder and onto my shirt and the ground in front of me as we approach the tunnel. Thomas stops suddenly and turns around. "Imani girl." He cups my face in his hands and kisses my lips gently. Then he pulls back. I can just make out his smile in the light.

"What?"

"Nothing. That's what." He turns, heading for the light and waves a bit before calling, "Too-da-loo, pretty. I'll be right back."

I smile and head left toward the main hall. I can't contain my hopes. My heart beats rapidly, and my cheeks feel flushed. I have no reason to run, but I can only slow to a quick walk. My mother isn't dead, and there is a chance she is *here* in the same mountain I am hiding in. The possibility is overwhelming— living a safe and free life with my mother. I always envisioned myself alone and free, or with my family and miserable.

I turn a corner too quickly and run right into someone else.

"Oomph!" I sprawl backwards, landing hard on my back-side and scraping my elbow.

"Oh!" a boy cries as he stumbles, barely catching himself. He is at my side in an instant, offering me his hand. "Beg your pardon."

I reach up and take hold of his rough palm, letting him hoist me to my feet.

"I'm so sorry." I rub my elbow and wipe the dirt from my skirt.

"My fault entirely. Y'all right?" he asks.

"Yes, I'm fine. Thank you," I say.

"Good." He nods and smiles then makes his way down the corridor again. I watch him for a minute before I realize he is dressed in the same clothes as the guards who'd gone to find my mother.

"Wait!" I cry and jog after him down the passageway.

"Yes?" He seems to be in a hurry but is polite enough to stop and answer.

"Do you know anything about the search party returning?" I ask, hopeful.

"Search party?"

"Yes, it went out a few weeks ago—Peter and James were heading it up, I believe."

"Oh right! You didn't hear? That was just a joke they played on that flatlander girl." The boy chuckles and adjusts the rifle on his back. "I've been trying to catch a glimpse of her for weeks. Have you seen her?"

My mouth is suddenly dry. "Joke?" *Flatlander girl? He doesn't recognize me.* I self-consciously touch the red hat still covering my hair. It is the only thing that sets me apart from the other girls with their short-cropped heads.

"Right good one too. They say she's plumb crazy because the Leaders pumped her head full of secrets. She came down here all throwing fits about going back out to the Institute to get her dead mum, but instead of locking her up and extracting the info, they decided to calm her down by telling her they sent a *search party* for her mum. Brilliant, if you ask me. Peter and James were due some leave, so they've been out at the hot pots for a while. Worked out like a charm."

The flow of words lands like bricks on my heart. I realize he is hoping I'll be impressed. Instead, I struggle to breathe.

"Yes, a fine joke," I manage to get out as I turn away from him.

He is still talking as I walk down the corridor toward my room, but I can't hear anything he says. All I can hear is Thomas's voice telling me to trust him, to trust Joe, not to approach the guards when we first saw them, not to bother Joe about it, that Thomas would take care of it.

*Trust.* Such a loaded word. How can I trust anyone? It is time to take matters into my own hands.

# SIXTEEN

I close and bolt the heavy wooden door to my room. My bedside lamp spills warm light on the small trunk they've given me to hold my things. I open it carefully, my hands shaking, and take out a pad of paper and a small stick of charcoal.

My chest is tight and heaving as I try to decide where I can sit to concentrate. The chair is too uncomfortable, the floor is too cold, and sitting on the bed is awkward.

"Oh, blast it," I swear as I grab the beautiful quilt and pillow off the bed and make myself a nest in the corner against the wall. I sit cross-legged on one corner of the quilt, facing the door, and wrap the rest of it around my shoulders. Instinctively, I begin to rock front to back. I close my eyes and hold the notebook close to my chest, trying to protect it from the large salty tears that are spilling down my face.

My mind bounces between Thomas laughing and kissing me and the words of the boy in the passageway—*just a joke they played on that flatlander girl.*

How can he do this? Did he know? He must have known.

That must have been why he didn't want me to talk to Joe or the guards on my own. Was he that desperate for me to stay in the mountain and become a member of his community? I keep thinking about the guards above ground. We could have made up a reason to talk to them, a reason for us to be out there. But he kept telling me no. He kept telling me not to talk to Joe. He had to have known.

I have to stop guessing and break down the facts. I am the "she" they were talking about in the council room. I know the truth, but they don't know I know. That gives me power—for a little time anyway. I don't know if Thomas was in on it or not, but if he was and I confront him, it will only make things worse and I'll lose the upper hand. If he wasn't, then I'll find that out eventually. Right now I need a plan and I need to act fast. I pick up a corner of the quilt and hesitate before wiping my streaming face on it.

It is so beautiful, so colorful and warm. That's how the mountain people seem as well—warm, caring, beautiful. Until you get to know them.

"I hate you!" I say out loud as I pinch my nose between two folds of the quilt and blow, hard. Then I take a deep breath, close my eyes, and get the paper and charcoal ready.

If they aren't going to get my mother, then I will. And the first thing I need to know is how to get back to the Institute.

I clear my mind and focus on my memory of the white building on the snowy, wooded hillside. I haven't tried to pull something this specific before. I don't even know if I have the information I need stored in my brain. I've seen glimpses of maps and diagrams behind the bright colors and sounds, but I've never really focused on them before.

At first, there's nothing. It's like my mind is battering itself against a wall—on one side is me and my memories, and on the other is the world's information. Sweat beads on my forehead but I don't bother to wipe it. I know there are cracks in this wall, and I have to find them.

I take a deep breath and think of nothing, and suddenly the wall evaporates and the deluge hits. My head begins to throb as images, flashes of light, and voices course through my mind in ever shorter bursts. I start to push it all back but check myself and focus on relaxing. I focus on my breath, letting myself immerse in the information instead of fighting to stay afloat. As soon as it surges over me, I realize I can still think as myself. The pain is gone and I can pull information at will from the flow around me if I concentrate.

*White building, maps, mountains, diagrams, archives...* I try to think of anything that might trigger the information. Slowly a stream of images starts to fill my mind—like the moving pictures of the film I projected on the wall of the Secondary School. Mentally, I push through ancient buildings long since crumbled to dust, military plans for structures deep underground—abandoned and left to fill with water. I find my way to more recent landscapes. Plans for pods, trains, a map of the

Leader's capital city.

*It must be here.* I had no idea there was such architectural variation, and I feel as if I could be sorting through building pictures forever. How can I narrow my search? Because the Institute is a Blue Spider rebel base, it may not even exist in the information I was given. Why would the Alliance pass on their secret files and plans to me? But it does also have use to the Leaders who think it's a Mind Wipe facility, so maybe there'll be something about that in this brain of mine.

After another few minutes of maps of government buildings built by the Leaders, I come across one labeled Mind Wipe Facility 1. I pause on it, studying its layout, but it's far larger than the Institute, and I mentally flip to the next diagram. I finally find it, identifying it by the river that runs next to it, its wooded location, and its layout with dorm rooms along the outside walls. It is labeled "Research and Development Institute."

I shift my mind to search geographic maps, knowing I cannot find my own way back to the Institute. I try not to dwell on the fact I will be making this journey alone.

A barrage of maps enters my mind, shifting by faster and faster. Some are from places I've never heard of, some more familiar, like the capitol and the farming communities around my home. There is even a map of the train system and the secondary school community. Soon I've got it narrowed down to maps of mines with a large river—which still leaves me with quite a few options. One diagram in particular matches what I remember from my trek with Thomas to the mines: a stream flowing into a larger river, clearly marked entrances to mines, a mountain-top village. I scan it closer, focusing on the stream—there are no mine entrances near it, just as I hoped. The door I entered with Thomas is still unknown to the Leaders and likely unknown to Hamen.

Suddenly I'm more determined, less helpless. I actually used the information shoved in my brain for something useful. I redouble my efforts and mentally scan the details, following the river upstream and looking for structures. There is nothing marked, so the Institute must be a secret location, or I'm looking at a map from before it was built. I begin scanning for trails and roads. A thin line snakes alongside the river on the far side of the bank, scissoring close then far away from it as it winds its way to the head waters. I open my eyes and make notes on what I saw. I gauge the distance from the mine entrance to the river and then to the trail or road on the other side and the bend in the river where I'm guessing the institute is.

I close my eyes again and decide to search for any information on the Blue Spider Alliance. There must be something in my memories connected to them. The more I know, the better prepared I will be. Without any more focus than the name of the revel group, I let my thoughts roam.

I find myself in my childhood pod. My mother's hand, outstretched, shoves a gray handkerchief into my own hand, a blue spider carefully sewn to its hem.

"Take it," she says.

I freeze the moment. I step outside myself and look at her sickly, gray face. I am drawn into her pain and suffering. I want to yell at her for not telling me sooner, for leaving me to find my way this far alone. But I break down sobbing instead and feel myself ripped back to the small room in the mine.

I grasp the notebook, pulling it to my chest, letting the charcoal smear on my clothes and arms, and I cry. Deep, racking sobs fill me and spill out into the solitary space—no longer in prison, but still not free. I cry for my mother, my brother's betrayal, my father's ignorance, and my confusion. I cry for my childishness and for the long road that still lies ahead. Eventually I lie on my side, using the wet quilt for a pillow. I roll myself deep into its folds and let the sobs die quietly as I drift into fitful sleep.

Rapping on the thick wood of my door startles me awake. I push myself off the floor, feeling stiff and achy.

"Imani? Are you in there?" Thomas's voice carries clearly through the wood. "Imani, love, I've been looking for you."

I didn't take the time to think this part through. What am I going to say to him? I don't know if I can even look at him again without crying, and that will ruin everything. One minute I feel empowered over the control I have with the information in my head, and the next I'm blubbering like a baby. I wonder if this is what it feels like to have a nervous breakdown.

"Are you okay?" He sounds genuinely concerned, which pulls at my heart, making me feel like a traitor to my mother.

I bang my fist on the wall and bite my lower lip. I have to do something; I can't hide in here. I decide a partial truth is the best way to handle the situation. Smoothing my hair and dress, I stand up, letting the quilt fall in a heap to the floor. The red hat sits lifeless next to it.

What if I hadn't worn it? Where would I be right now? Would I still be hanging on their lies?

I slowly step to the door. "Who is it?"

A stupid question. I know exactly who is waiting on the other side.

"It's Thomas. Imani, are you doing all right in there?"

I slide the lock back slowly and peer into the corridor, into his face.

His eyes are laced with genuine concern and confusion. "I found Joe. He had news for you. Although prolly not the news you were hoping for. That's why they waited to tell you."

"I already know."

"What? How?"

I feel terrible about having to lie to him, but he's misled me first. It's time to weave my tale. "I ran into a guard on my way to the cafeteria. He said they returned without her."

"Aw, sweets. I'm so sorry. Did he tell you anything else?"

*He could be telling the truth, but it's more likely he's fish-*

*ing for information. He wants to know how much I know so he can adjust his story. I can do this. I can play this game.*

"Just that they couldn't get her out." I hiccup on the last word, emotion bubbling up inside me.

"Joe said they couldn't even confirm she was at that facility."

I nod and he reaches for me.

I can't do it.

I turn my face away from him. "I'm not feeling well. I just need to be alone for a while."

He stops, obviously surprised. And a little hurt. "Alrighty, I can see that. Can I bring you something? Are you thirsty or hungry?"

Now that he mentions it, I am very thirsty, but I shake my head—*no.*

He frowns.

I step back to close the door again.

"Imani," he steps closer and puts his hand on the door, keeping me from closing it.

I look up at him, barely able to keep my tears under control.

"It's not so bad living here. I know you miss your ma and all, but really, it's not so bad. The folks like you, and I've got hope for you and me. We have a chance down here."

"Yeah, I know." It is barely a whisper, but it is all I can get out as I close the door all the way and slide the bolt into place.

Thomas doesn't stop me.

# SEVENTEEN

The next few days go by in a blur. I spend most of my time helping in the classroom answering as many questions as I can and telling the history of our people at story time. The teachers seem to genuinely like me and get excited when I recall something I can add to their lessons. Adelaide still avoids me, but she's less openly hostile which makes the situation easier to bear. It is such a strange feeling to be in school and also be both accepted and encouraged to talk— I almost enjoy it.

Thomas is back at work deep in the mines, so I don't see him much, which I'm glad of. Maire and her disappointment are a lot harder to avoid. And for some reason, everywhere I go, even outside of the classroom, I run into Adelaide. But every dirty look or hard bump from her shoulder as she passes me sets my mind more firmly to my plans.

I'm given one day a week off of helping, so I choose to leave early on that morning. I hope no one will be suspicious if they don't see me for a while. It was easy enough to lie about not feeling well when Thomas and I missed a day together, but it would be much harder this time.

I don't sleep at all the night before. I know I will be tired, but I want to make sure I am awake and ready to go at first light. Unlike the school, which had clocks, and the prison, which had scheduled lights that came on during the day and shut off at night, the private rooms in the tunnels have no clocks and very few electronics to speak of. I suppose I could have requested an alarm clock, but it's too late for that.

I spend the long dark hours in my room, afraid to turn on the light and draw attention, mentally going through the images in my mind—the maps, what food I will take, the warm clothing I need to find. I still have the red hat tucked neatly into a small rucksack. I lie in my bed, holding the sack with both hands, thinking about all the other nights like this in my life, and wondering if this attempt will be successful.

It seems as if running away is becoming my thing.

Thinking about the past attempts makes me think about Thomas. And thinking about Thomas, even his betrayal, makes me think about his lips.

I groan and roll to my side, clutching the sack like a small one holds their favorite blanket. I still can't make myself hate him. Anger, distrust, and disappointment flood my heart when I think of him, but I can't shake the feeling of his arms around me, capable and strong, and his breath warming me just before he nibbles my neck and ear. Thomas's open smile and his deceit don't seem like they could come from the same body.

Goosebumps dance down my arms in spite of the warm quilt. I want desperately to sneak to his room and call him out. I want to know what he thought he was going to do with me, how long he thought he could hide the truth, and how he thought I'd react when I found out.

Maybe he is using me to make his family uptight and his bride-to-be jealous. Maybe he is still planning on marrying her after the council is done with me. But none of these ideas match the Thomas I know.

"What a mess," I whisper and sigh. I can't help wishing we were back in the little house, curled together and talking in the minutes before I saw his sister at the window.

If I'm wrong, it will crush him.

Maybe I can go to his room. Maybe he doesn't know. Maybe I could tell him, and he will come with me and help me. Then I won't be so alone.

I start to rise from my bed, my heart bouncing against my ribs recklessly.

Then I remembered the words of the guard again—*just a joke they played on that flatlander girl.*

I shake my head and take a deep breath. If there is any chance he was in on this kind of joke, I don't think I can face it. Besides, I can do this alone. I've done a lot alone up until now. I don't *need* him. What I need is to find my mother and make sure she is all right. No one else is going to do that job for me.

I stand up, my desire to go to Thomas's room now replaced

with the determination to succeed. There are no more sounds of late night activities. It is earlier than I'd planned, but now is as good a time as any to slip out unnoticed.

I turn on the small lamp next to my bed and open the trunk of clothes Maire gave me. I get out my warmest socks and a pair of pants and pull them on under my night gown. Then I find a thick wool sweater and tug that on. It is long, hanging almost to my knees. It has deep pockets and I can easily hide the rucksack in its soft fuzzy folds. Plus, it is a creamy white color, like it had been recently lifted off a sheep, and it is the one thing besides the quilt that I want to take with me. The quilt will have to stay.

I lace up my boots and go back to the bed. I pull the corners of the blankets and sheets up, then run a hand down the soft cotton of the brightly colored quilt. It is everything beautiful I love about the mountain people, everything I dreamed about as a child. I straighten the corners as carefully as possible. Then I turn my back and walk out the door, closing it behind me,

Thomas's room is only a few doors down from mine. I've never actually been inside, but I know which one it is. I stare at the crack between the large panel of wood and the stone floor— no light. I don't allow myself to feel disappointed. I keep walking toward the kitchens. I planned to grab apples and bread as Thomas and I did the first time, but as I round the dimly lit corridor, I see a bright light shining in the pantry area. Small *clinks* and *thuds* of items being moved reach me.

I duck my head back and freeze against the wall. Who could

be up this late digging around with the lights on? How am I going to get my food?

I consider heading back down the corridor to the hidden stairs and doing the trip without food, but that puts a panicky feeling in my gut.

I peek around the corner again, and a shadow spills from the pantry onto the square of light on the floor. It is definitely a man. I can use an excuse, say that I am hungry, or just wait until he leaves.

But what if it's Thomas?

I listen carefully but hear nothing more than the shuffling and clinking of bottles. Thomas would have at least whistled a tune by now. I can't think of a time when Thomas has ever been completely silent, except for when we were hiding from someone. The boy is always talking or singing, humming or whistling. If it wasn't so cheery it would drive me insane.

I decide I can't wait any longer. There are no signs of this person leaving and I'm not going anywhere without at least a small meal.

I take a deep breath and step into the common room, making my way toward the bright yellow opening. As I draw closer, I slow down and consider saying something, just to avoid an awkward situation. But I am too late. Without turning off the light, a man in a night shirt and socks, arms full of food, walks right into me.

It's Joe.

# EIGHTEEN

"**O**h!" Joe jumps a little, dropping an apple to the cold stone floor. He bends to pick it up, balancing the rest of his load awkwardly in his arms. "I didn't expect to see you here, Imani."

"I'm sorry," I answer, willing him to feel embarrassed and leave quickly.

Instead, he stands up and faces me. "You are up late. Did you miss dinner as well?" He laughs at his own joke and indicates with a nod the bread, cheese, and newly bruised apple in his arms.

I don't want to lie. Lying always leads to more questions, and I don't want to have to keep track of my answers.

"No, I just want a midnight snack." I try to walk around him, forcing a smile.

"I suppose you are still a growing girl." He looks at me closely, following me with his eyes as I pass, taking in more than just my baggy sweater and loose hair. I can tell he has something he wants to say, and I'm not sure I want to hear it.

"Imani." He draws out each letter, making me shudder.

*Don't say my name like that,* I think. I stand in the pantry door way, take a deep breath of the dark air, and turn to face him.

He takes a step toward me. "You've been here for quite a while now and we've never really had the chance to speak privately. How are you doing?"

I take a step back, deeper into the pantry. "I guess I'm doing all right."

He sets his food down on a nearby table and put his hands on his hips. "I know your life hasn't been easy, but I want to make sure you know that you are welcome here." He pauses again. "Despite what you may have heard from some of our citizens."

"If you are talking about Adelaide, I'm not worried." I try to turn away to signal that this conversation is over. But he reaches out and grabs my arm, his hand gentle but firm. And it isn't until this moment that I realize just how strong he is for a man only slightly larger than myself.

"Well, Adelaide and others." He takes another step toward me, holding me in place with one hand as he reaches up and runs his other hand down my other shoulder and upper arm.

The motion, the contact, confuses me. What is he doing?

"There's a place for you here. I know you think you are alone in this world, but you aren't. I've been watching you. You are good with the students and there are plenty of people who like you, even though you are different." He lingers on the last word as he reaches up and touches my hair, running a piece through his fingers from scalp to tip.

I freeze. This is not something I expected. If this were Thomas, it would feel good, natural, but everything feels wrong when Joe touches me. I look at him, making sure my imagination isn't fooling me.

He smiles and I feel worse. I will myself to do something, say something. But what?

"Imani, I like you. I like you very much. I have since the first day you arrived. I know that you have spent a lot of time with Thomas, and he is a wonderful young man, but he is betrothed and has a place and a future already made for him. You are free. You can do whatever you like here." He waves his arm to capture the giant room where our hushed voices bounce off the walls.

Then he focuses his dark eyes on me again, and I feel the walls of the pantry are closing in on me. "My betrothed died in the raids. I need a new partner. I need a smart woman like you to help me lead these people. You've seen the outside world. You know what it's like. We are headed into tough times. War is imminent. I need a woman I can trust and count on. Beauty is just a bonus." He smiles again and touches my cheek.

Flashbacks of the guard who attacked me in my cell, more powerful than any of Hamen's information, wash over me. My guts twist and I might throw up all over his night shirt. This man who has lied to me about my mother and is twice my age hopes to win me over by telling me I'm beautiful while he stands before me in his nightshirt. Does he know how ridiculous he looks? How ridiculous he sounds? And yet his confident smiles and the firm way his large hand holds my arm tell me he is completely serious.

"Um" is all I can manage to push out in response.

"I know you probably didn't expect this, but this surprise encounter—it seemed the perfect moment to discuss a partnership with you." He pulls me to him with eager eyes and hands.

My stomach lurches as I resist his pull. He actually thinks I will reciprocate?

"Joe, you are old enough to be my grandfather." I step back, knocking into a shelf behind me.

"That doesn't matter here." He steps closer again, and I lean back as much as possible. "We do not base our relationships on age. We do not formulate and plan unions the way you might think. We have choice and the eldest get to choose first. I've been waiting for the right woman all these months. And you are exactly who I want."

He leans in like Thomas does when he is about to kiss me. Only, instead of meeting Joe halfway, I duck under his arm and shrug off his grip. Is this why he didn't want Thomas at the meeting? Has he been trying to get me alone?

"Joe, this is not what I'm looking for." I try to keep my voice level, knowing he can make life hell for me down here. Despite his lies about my mother and who knows what else, he is still in charge. And he is still standing between me and the door to my mother. All he has to do is yell for the guards and accuse me of something, and I'll be locked up all over again. I don't think he is that kind of man, but I've learned quickly never to underestimate someone's need for revenge. Better not to give them a reason to hate you.

"I'm not ready to *partner* with anyone." The word makes me even more nauseated, though I try to say it matter-of-factly.

He responds quietly, "Is it Thomas? Are you in love?"

I don't hesitate. "No, it's just that I'm so worried about my mother and war and what is going to happen to all of us. It just doesn't feel like the right time." I can't believe I am having this conversation with not only an adult, but the leader of the mountain people.

"I can respect that. We've done all we can to find your mother. I'm afraid that's a quest you may have to wait on."

I cringe at how sincere his lie is but keep my breathing steady. He can't know I've learned the truth. Not yet.

"I understand. I just... I still don't think this is a good time." I stand to the side of the pantry door, willing him to leave. "Plus I'm very tired, and I just want to grab a snack and go to sleep." I hold my breath, waiting for his response.

He lets his head hang for a moment. Is that dejection? Did I cause that tiredness to cascade over his face and body?

"I suppose you may be right. It is very late." He picks up his food and faces me. "I won't speak of this again. I'll leave it to you to come to me when you are ready."

I can't help it—I quiver at the thought of coming to him for anything after this. But I manage to nod and turn to the pantry, leaving him to walk away alone, grateful I didn't have to fight him off.

I try not to think about standing so close to him, feeling his hands on my hair and his eyes on my face, my body. Every time I do, I gag. I distract myself by focusing on finding food that will last a day in my pack. I find a small loaf of bread and a couple of apples. Under a cloth I find a fresh pie. It's large and smells so good, but I know I have nowhere to keep it for the long hike up river. I replace the cloth, grab a hunk of cheese, and fill a container with water, then stuff it all into the sack hidden in my sweater.

Before I flip the lights out, I check the common room to make sure Joe is really gone. The last thing I need is to run into him again. The room is clear, so I shut off the lights and pick my way carefully through the tables and chairs.

By now I've tread this path often enough that I don't need more than the ambient moonlight falling from the ceiling tubes to find my way. It feels good to know exactly where I am going from here. I fish a small portable light from my pack and hold it at the ready as I approached the supply closet. I will need it to find the right clothing.

A few steps more and the air starts to feel muggier. I'm coming up on the bathing chamber, which means the closet is close at hand. I switch on the light and see the door I need.

Inside I find a coat, gloves, and pair of lightweight snow pants. I pull off my nightdress and tuck it behind a box at the back of a shelf. I throw my pack over my shoulder, then turn to leave, ready to switch off my light again.

Propped next to the door, in the corner where no one would see it, is a gun.

I stare at the long, black, sinister-looking barrel. It is a shock rifle. I'd been hit by one when trying to escape the prison, so I know the damage it could do. I'd been lucky not to die. At least I had thought I was lucky.

I think about the weight of the gun, the distance I have to travel, the probability of needing to use it against wipers in the woods, and I swing it over my shoulder by the strap, flip off the light, and open the door.

# NINETEEN

The air in the stairway grows colder as I approach the exit to the surface. I pull on my hat and gloves as I climb and ready the light. There is no telling what time it is or how dark it will be outside.

A few minutes later, I reach the top of the stairs and can feel the large door to the village in front of me. I take hold of the handle and push as hard as I can, remembering how difficult it was to open before. It's stuck tight, so I shove again, bracing my feet against the rough floor. Suddenly, it swings open, knocking me back against the wall. Ice cold air blasts my face. I hold my breath as I struggle to regain my footing and climb outside. I can't afford to make too much noise or leave the door open too long.

Before me the forest is dark, but not so dark that I can't see. The almost full moon shines bright through the trees, leaving odd shapes of light and shadow on the ground. The snow sits in splotches here and there, dark, wet earth surrounding it. Spring thaw means no snowy footprints to worry about. I can avoid muddy ones by stepping on rocks and moss.

I secure the door behind me and set off through the trees. Thanks to my practice recalling it, the detailed map of the surrounding woodlands comes easily to mind. There is a small ravine to the north. I can follow it down the mountain to the river where I will head north again and eventually hit a bridge that spans the angry river.

The plan is simple: get as close as I can without getting caught. If I get caught, I turn myself in like Hamen asked. If I don't get caught, I try to break Mother out.

I don't think about how many things could go wrong.

The air grows colder as the night wears on. It is slow going along the ravine. The ground is rocky, and the bushes and trees grow thick on either side. I push through as quietly as I can. Guards could be anywhere.

Finally, the rocks give way to softer, more level earth. I figure I've been hiking for about an hour when I come upon a spring bubbling up from the rocks and flowing ahead of me to one side. It may be the same creek Thomas and I followed to find his home in the first place. I continue on for a few minutes more before I hear the rushing of the river before me. I keep pushing through the dark, and although the sound grows louder, the river doesn't reveal itself.

All at once the trees part and a bright patch of moonlight streams down before me, bouncing off the tossing waves and eddies that rush past below. I've made it.

My shoulders ache from carrying my knapsack and the

heavy gun. I shift the gun to my other side and find a log to sit on. It occurs to me that if I do get caught, I can blast my way through like a crazy person. But the idea of actually shooting someone makes me feel like throwing the long black shock stick in the river. My nerves still ache whenever I recall the time I'd been blasted.

Still, it's my only defense out here besides crawling under a bush, and I doubt that will actually work. I stand and stretch, then heft the gun back onto my shoulder—better safe than sorry.

The sky along the tops of the mountains is just beginning to turn from midnight black to deep purple. Morning is coming, and I still have several miles to walk before I can rest again. I step back into the thick trees, away from the rushing current. I need to be able to hear my surroundings as I go. I congratulate myself on having not run across anyone thus far. It is another small miracle.

How much better this trek would be with Thomas next to me. I try not to think about being in his arms, laughing with him, kissing him. Instead I focus on my mother and what it will be like to see her again, to hold her, to kiss her and feel her breath on my head and her soft fingers braiding my hair like when I was young. Is she well? Were there lasting effects from the illness? Is she even at the Institute? I had no doubt she was alive when they took that photo. Her face, her smile, her sparkling eyes are all the same—but touched by tiny lines that weren't there before. She looked tired, older.

In spite of her aging, she also looks happy. Did Hamen take the picture himself? I wonder how much she knows. Is she willingly joining Hamen's cause? If that's the case, then maybe I will too. It would be better to be with her and negotiate his crazy than be apart again and with people I don't trust.

The thought of being somewhere with my mother that doesn't include an autoeye spying on us makes my chest grow tight. We can embrace and laugh and discuss anything we want without whispering and looking over our shoulders or bracing for a reprimand. No one will take away our strawberry allotment for an illegal sign of affection.

Hot tears well up and stream down my cheeks. The cold mountain air catches them and quickly turns the wet patches into freezing streaks of salt. I hike harder, more determined, and wipe my face with a gloved hand. The only way to find the answer to any of these questions is to get there alive.

I focus on recalling the plans for the institute. In my time outside of class and avoiding Thomas, I've come up with two plans for getting in and out of the building based on the single diagram I've been able to find of it. I go over the diagram and my access routes as I walk.

The sun rises above the tree line and lights the world around me with golden sparkles. My spirits lift considerably as I trudge through the beautiful landscape, each step bringing me closer to my goal. The occasional bird sings and trees creak, but other than that, nothing disturbs my march.

I pause for a snack and to rest my shoulders from the weight of the rifle. A tree fallen on the edge of a large meadow seems the perfect place to rest awhile and eat. I take small bites and deep breaths. It's pure bliss—quiet, empty, and sunlit. I'm tempted to lie down in the middle of the clearing like I used to do in the Fields of Yesterday back in my home community. But I can't give up the shelter of the trees. My experience tells me that if I take the chance and spread myself out in the open, a guard will appear.

A movement across the clearing catches my eye. I stand up and grab the rifle, sidestepping to the edge of the log and back into the trees. There is a good chance I am paranoid. There's also a good chance that if someone is there, they've already seen me.

Another movement confirms my suspicions. I'm not crazy. Something is definitely fifty feet away from me in the dark undergrowth of the forest.

I shoulder my bag and pull the rifle up to a firing position. I carefully place my finger on the trigger and aim at a branch that is now moving constantly as whatever it is moves closer to the clearing.

"What in the world?" I whisper to myself as I realize it must be someone crawling. The movement is low to the ground and vigorous. If they are trying to sneak up on me, the attempt is failing miserably.

I keep my eyes focused on the spot and take a deep breath,

my finger barely tightening on the trigger, ready to squeeze the second I have to.

Suddenly a boar bursts through the branches and into the clearing. I jump and pull the trigger, sending a shot of electricity flying into the tree tops above the pig's head. It squeals and races farther into the clearing, four squealing piglets follow behind her.

I drop the rifle tip and lean against the nearest tree, taking a deep breath. It's harsh realizing that if that had been an actual guard set on capturing me, I'd either be dead or in handcuffs right now. What good is the gun if I can't even fire it straight?

Once again, I consider leaving it behind. It is heavy and slows me down. I don't know how to fire it correctly. Even if I did, I don't know if I could fire it under pressure. Actually, now I know I can't fire it under pressure.

I set the gun down and readjust my pack. I take a few steps forward without it, then double back and pick it up again. Even though it is ridiculous, I can't just leave my only weapon behind. I could at least use it as a visual deterrent. Other people don't know I can't shoot it.

School drilled into our heads that you could prepare for almost anything by thinking through it step by step and deciding in advance how you would respond to any issue that might arise. I shoulder the rifle and begin hiking again, only this time I imagine myself in all kinds of ambush situations, flipping the gun over quickly and hitting my target with no hesitation. Calm, steady hand. Sure aim, perfect control of my index finger. I can do this.

The sun arcs across the sky as I continue to hike, and soon it's disappearing over the mountains. According to my calculations, I am drawing nearer to the rockiest part of the journey, and just beyond that is the bridge and a lookout camp. I pick up my pace as the light fades. The trees dwindle and rocks replace them, creating steep cliffs on either side of the river.

I sling the straps for my bag and the rifle over my head and across my chest, so I can lean forward and use my hands and legs to scale the ascent. It is painfully slow going and light is fading quickly. I have to make it to the other side before dark or there is a chance that I will fall.

The top of the outcropping draws closer as the light fades into brown shadows. My arms and legs burn with exertion, but I am going to make it. I come within an easy five feet of the top and decide to rest on a ledge and catch my breath. I make sure my seating is solid before I lean back on my pack and gun and take a deep breath. My water bottle is almost empty, but I know there is a brook on this side of the river before the bridge. I gulp down the rest of my water and let the cool night settle in around me.

A star twinkles and shines just over my head. I am so close, and the night is so beautiful, I almost don't hear the rock fall below me. I sit up and peer through the dark to the ledges below. It could be another animal. I'd seen a few more boar throughout the day and saw deer tracks. I can't imagine either climbing a rock face like this in the dark of night. Maybe it is a goat.

I force myself to see small horns on a furry head below me. But the light, although waning, is still present enough to reveal the top of a human head, covered in a guard cap, followed by a hand reaching up to the next ledge.

I scramble up the last few feet of incline. At the top I look for a place to hide. All my mental preparation from the hours before rush at me like a flood. A large boulder stands to one side of my ascension spot. I scurry around it and pull the rifle strap over my head, positioning myself with the barrel pointing over the top of the rock at whomever is coming.

They must have the same goal as me: get over the rocks before dark. I can hear them carelessly scrambling as the light fades from brown to black and nothing but the stars shine above the deep dark mountain side. The moon hasn't risen yet.

If I stay calm and keep the gun on the rock, I should be able to shoot whoever comes above the ridge before they even know what hit them. Even if there is more than one guard down there, I can take them out.

I repeat this to myself for what feels like an hour but is probably only five minutes, until movement disturbs the edge of the rock. I hear a grunt and a scrape of body on gravel. Whoever's there just pulled themselves over the side.

I close my eyes and count to ten, giving them time to stand up, making my target as large as possible. I hear a grunt and more scraping and then open my eyes to the moon outlining the definite form of a large man.

*Now or never,* I think.

I aim carefully, take a deep breath, and pull the trigger.

Light from the black barrel tears through the night, finding it's mark in the center of the man's chest. For a split second I can see his face, and his eyes meet mine. He lets out a primal scream on impact.

"Imani!"

And so do I.

"Thomas!"

# TWENTY

I drop the gun and clamber over the rock, stumbling until I am at Thomas's side. Luckily his fall was broken by a large boulder—otherwise he could've tumbled a good ways down the mountain face. I wrap my arm under his head and whisper his name over and over. "Thomas, what are you doing here? How did you find me?" I run my hand over his chest. It is hot in the darkness, and charred bits of his clothing show where it is singed from the blast. "Thomas?"

He doesn't respond.

"I'm so sorry," I whisper as my chest tightens, fearing the worst.

I look up, scanning the trees and rocks, as if someone might appear to help us. But we are completely alone.

"Thomas!" Panic takes over and I shake him. His body is heavy and limp—too limp. I let his head rest on the ground and press my ear down on his chest.

His chest isn't rising and falling. His clothing is too thick to hear a heartbeat. I pull at the zipper on his burnt coat, throwing it wide to the twilight air. Then I carefully start work on the buttons of his soft blue shirt. My hands shake in the damp cold and I fumble as tears run down my cheeks.

"Thomas, what were you thinking? How did you even know I was out here?" I whisper as I lay my head on his chest, listening for life. I don't care why he's out here, but I need to hear something in this terrible silence.

"I was thinking you're not very good at sneaking around, and there are much easier ways to get my clothes off of me."

I lurch backward with a yelp. "You're not dead!"

"Thank the sun and moon and your bad aim—no, I am not dead."

I scramble back to his side, knowing the pain he must be in, and try to help him sit up. "What are you doing out here?" My indignation lingers, but only just.

"I'd like to ask the same of you." He rubs his temple then looks at me, hard. "You slip slide around me for days and then all the sudden skip out without even a goodbye. Not very lady-like, my love."

The last words shoot from his mouth without their usual affection. I stiffen and sit back on my heels. All the elation I felt at him being alive withers under his almost accusatory glare.

"What do you want?"

"I came to try and keep you from turning yourself back over to those loonies."

"Who says I'm turning myself in?" I cross my arms and feel righteous indignation fill me. He doesn't know what I know.

"Well, what else are you planning with that pretty little head? Hmm? You going to break your ma out on your own?"

I stand and walk back to my pack. If Thomas isn't going to try to understand where I'm coming from, I won't bother trying to explain. Part of me wants to lose my cool, aches to scream at him—*Why did you lie to me? Why didn't you tell me they weren't going to look for my mother? Why did you lead me on?*

But a bigger, stronger part of me just wants to see my mother again. And I hate to admit it, but I still care for Thomas. I shoulder my pack and lift the shock rifle to a ready position, barrel pointed at to the sky, before turning back to him.

"Listen, I know you're under some sort of orders to keep an eye on me, and I know the council wants me to cough my brains out onto a table for them to dissect and make use of, but I have to take care of my mother. You don't understand what it means to me that she is still alive. I have to see her, and since none of you want to help me do that, I'm going to do it on my own."

Thomas laughs, then cringes and shakes his head. "You daft, daft girl. You think that if the council knew you were out here, traipsing right into the hands of the enemy, that they'd send me to bring you back? Ho, no. There'd be a whole team of burly big arms out here, and you'd already be in a bag kicking your way back under the mountain."

"Then what do you want?" I shrug the pack onto my shoulder.

"I just want to know that you're all right. Lass, you drive

me bonkers! One minute you're hot as a winter fire, the next I can't get you to open your door. Then you pop out in the middle of the night like a ferret. What's a man supposed to think?"

He struggles to stand up and I instinctively reach out to help. As he clasps my hand, he looks me in the eye and says softly, "Something's changed. I want to know what that is. I think I have a right to know."

If this is an act, it is a very good one. I can feel my resolve starting to falter as I pull him up to stand. I want to trust him, but my priority right now is rescuing Mother. I can repair bridges with Thomas later.

"Thomas, a lot has happened—"

"In three days?"

"Yes. No, I mean, it's been happening for a while, but I just put it all together."

"What did you put together? Just tell me." He squeezes my hand gently.

I shake my head and pull my hand from his. "I don't have time to stand around here and hash this out with you. I have to get to the Institute before it's too dark so I can scout it out and make a plan. I don't know what you are going to do, but I'm not going back with you until I see Mother."

"So you really are just going to waltz up there alone and try to get your ma out." Thomas looks down and shakes his head. Then he looks back up at me. "And you're really not going to tell me what the hell happened?"

"No. I'm leaving. What are you going to do?"

He folds his arms and squares his shoulders. "If you're not going to tell me, then I'm not going to tell you."

"Fine." I turn to go.

"But I'll give you a hint. It has something to do with the guard station just over the hill."

I keep walking and call over my shoulder, "If you turn me in, they'll just throw you back in prison too."

"Not that guard station—the rebel one. The one that's full of my folk. Remember? The big armed guys?"

I stop, confusion and suspicion making me narrow my eyes. "There's no guard post over the hill."

"And how would you know, Miss My-brain-is-only-full-of-poetry?"

"What do you mean?" I ask.

"You think I don't know that you've been lying to the council all this time? I've seen you have those episodes about all sorts of things—not just artsy stuff. Your head is so full of everything you can't hide it—at least not from me."

"I wasn't trying to hide anything. I just didn't know how to deal with it, or who I could trust."

"And you thought you couldn't trust me?" he says.

"Honestly, I've been a bit doubtful of that in the past few days," I say, a lump building in my throat.

"But you'll trust all that knowing that came from them?" He points out to the plains. "The flatlanders don't know everything there is to know about us. Especially where our outposts may or may not be."

"You're bluffing." I don't flinch at his threats, but my heart droops. If there are hidden mountain guard outposts this far out, there is no way I can get past them in these foothills, and that means there is no way I can get anywhere near my mother. They'd haul me back to the mountain and lock me up tighter than the government prison, then probably torture me to get at the information in my head. The thought of that threatens to make me panic, but I keep my breathing calm and steady. It hasn't happened yet.

"Am I? Walk away from me and see for yourself." He buttons up his shirt slowly, knowing I'm watching.

"What do you want?"

In three large steps he is standing in front of me, a hand on each of my arms. He looks carefully at my face, his own brow wrinkled in serious concern. "Just tell me what happened, and I'll let you go." Then he adds quickly, "Or I'll help you, if that's what you want. Only don't just leave me like that without saying anything."

Whatever strength left inside me melts in his hands. I am so tired of going in circles. Longing for things to return to the way they were takes over my thoughts and forces the words out of me. "You lied to me."

It is only a whisper, but we are close enough that he heard.

"I did no such thing. What are you talking about?" He looks

genuinely confused.

I frown, looking for the lie in his face, but he meets my eyes honestly. If he is acting, he is evil. If he genuinely doesn't know… then I've wasted precious time and resources. Nothing is going as planned.

I clench my hands into fists at my side. "You all lied to me. They told me they went after my mother and couldn't find her, but they didn't. No one went anywhere. The guards they sent laid around some rest area until it was time to pretend they were back from scouting. No one did anything, Thomas." Instead of feeling better to have it all out, I feel angrier. "And if you tell me you didn't know, I'll have a very hard time believing that, Mr. Future-leader-of-the-clan."

My voice rings in the still evening air. I shouldn't have shouted. If there really is a post over the hill, I've given away my location and this whole conversation will get me in more trouble. But I can't help it. I feel like I am going to explode.

Thomas rubs a hand over his eyes. "What a mess. Who told you any of this? How did you put this together?" When I open my mouth to reply, he puts a finger to my lips. "But keep it down, lass, or you'll get yourself locked up without my help."

I nod and he removes his finger. "A guard told me the night you went to find Joe." Now my words are almost too soft. Thomas listens intently. "He thought I was someone else. He was laughing about it, Thomas. It's been a joke for weeks now—fooling the flatlander girl." I choke up at the last words and look away. I hate myself for being weak, but I can't help it.

"Imani," he says as he squeezes my arms. "Look at me, love."

I feel like a sucker, but I do as he asks and look up at him through my tears.

"We're going to figure this out together. Do you understand? I wasn't a part of any joke. They played me for as much a fool as they played you. Are you hearing me?"

I nod. I believe him.

"Good." He shakes his head and sighs. "No wonder you shot me as soon as you got the chance. I'd have shot me too. Those bleeding bastards. I was afraid they'd pull something like this. I don't quite understand all they've got going on, but this new information you're handin' out gives me a pretty good idea."

"What do you mean?" It's my turn to feel confused.

"There's war brewing and I have a feeling you are more important to their plans than they let on."

"So you're not going to hand me over?"

"You're the one with the gun." He smiles a wide grin and takes me into his arms, gun and all.

And I let him.

# TWENTY ONE

Tromping through the dark woods with Thomas at my side brings a sense of calm I haven't felt in days. I told him he didn't have to come with me, but he quieted me with another kiss then gestured for me to lead the way. As we walk, he points out several instances where my plan may not hold together but offers solutions to help get the job done. I would have walked right into the secret guard station he warned me about had I not come across him when I did. I'm so grateful I tell him too many times and he finally threatens me.

"Lassie, you say *thank you* or *I'm sorry* one more time and I'm gonna lose it. This is what you do when you love someone."

I gulp down fresh tears. "I love you too."

We circumnavigate the guard post and the bridge leading up to it. Instead, he tells me about an old rope bridge just a mile farther up the river. We cut low and head upstream in silence until we come to the massive ropes tied to a large tree on our side of the rushing current and a twin on the opposite bank.

"Grab hold of this rope up here, and step lightly on this rope down here," he says.

Thomas is explaining the finer points of double rope bridges as I look on in terror. My mind flashes scenes of men falling to their deaths when a crossing just like this was cut from one side, or a misplaced foot and unsure handhold sent them plummeting like a big rock into the swirling currents below.

"Do ya want me to go first?" He looks at me expectantly.

"I'm not sure you could do much to help me if you were in front or behind." I study the wet, sagging old ropes.

"Fair enough. I'll go first and carry the pack so you aren't off balance."

I take a deep breath and drop the pack on the ground. I sling the rest of the gun strap across my chest and notice Thomas eyeing it.

"You know that probably weighs more than the pack, right?"

I considered his observation and look back at the pack. He is right. And in his own careful way, he is trying to see if I still trust him.

I slowly lift the strap back over my head and hand it to him. He steps closer to take it and leans in to kiss me.

"It's going to be all right." He smiles and shoulders both the pack and the gun, securing the straps over his head. He grabs the upper rope and steps onto the lower.

"Ready?"

I nod and follow his lead, pausing to take off my gloves to get a better grip on the thick rope. We inch over the river, hand over hand, foot over foot.

It is very slow going. Spray from the white water below makes the twisted fibers slippery. The rough, wet surface soon tears into my soft palms, but at least I'm making progress. The chill of night makes me shiver as my fingers gradually lose feeling.

The water below makes such a roaring sound I almost don't catch the light bouncing trill at first. But above the crashing water, I pick out a distinct sound: Thomas is whistling.

My fear starts to trickle away. Each step seems easier and the far shore approaches more rapidly. As we come within a couple of feet of the bank, Thomas springs for land. Then he turns to me and holds out his hands.

The moon has risen, full and beaming down on his smiling face. Only Thomas would be happy at a time like this, having just crossed a river from one place where we're most likely being hunted to another where we are definitely about to be hunted.

"Here we go," he says as I reach for him and he lifts me easily to the bank above. "Now, miss, where to?"

I take a step away from the water's edge and look around, thinking about the maps I'd accessed. I signal for him to follow me up the bank. A few steps up the incline the land levels off to a forest like the one we just left. I turn around to help Thomas up, but he is already standing behind me.

"I believe the Institute is just a few hundred yards that

way." I point back down the river and through the trees. "I'm hoping the guards stay close to the institute itself and if we travel along the bank, we should avoid them."

"I believe you are right as a rainbow. Let's get going."

I take the lead and head into the trees as he adjusts the pack and the gun then follows.

I stop and wait for him, suddenly wanting his hand in mine, when a dark figure bounds from the trees, shrieking as it tackles me. I hit the ground hard and we roll over the edge of the bank, back toward the river. Strong fingers dig into my arms and whoever or whatever it is howls with pain as we slam together against a rock. Luckily, I'm on top, and the impact shakes the creature's grip on me. I roll and land on a bush at the edge of the water, but the monster is on top of me a second later, snarling and growling. He shoves his face into my neck and lancing pain races through my body as I realize he is biting and pulling at the flesh of my shoulder.

"Thomas!"

No sooner has the name left my lips than a resounding *crack* fills the air. A shock jolts me into a moment of suspended reality, and then the monster man falls heavily on top of me, motionless.

I moan and try to catch my breath. Blood runs in a warm stream from my throbbing shoulder down my neck and pools behind my head.

"Imani!" Thomas is there, somewhere.

The weight on top of me lifts away. I hear a tearing and scraping noise then a splash and Thomas is at my side, digging through the pack and wiping my hair back from my face.

"Hold on, love," he says.

"He bit my shoulder," I say. The thought of the man's mouth tearing into my skin sends a new wave of sickness through me and I turn on my side and vomit.

# TWENTY TWO

"That was definitely the craziest wiper I've ever seen," Thomas says as he rips up a clean shirt to use as a bandage.

"I thought the Mind Wipe left you without any sort of desires or personality. That *thing* definitely wanted something," I say, shuddering.

"I sat in on a report the latest group of recon guards came in with a couple of days ago. I wanted to talk to you about it but couldn't ever catch up with you. They got word that even the ones whose minds were wiped the old-fashioned way are starting to have issues. They used to be mindless slobs that did whatever they were told. Lately more and more of them have been going a bit bonkers and—" He hesitates as he pats tenderly at my shoulder. "Developing a taste for their own kind."

My stomach twists and my head pounds as visions of teeth ripping flesh and staggering feet fill my mind. Zombies—that was the word used in the old days. Ancient culture was filled with references, movies, songs, cult followings—but no actual zombie was ever reported as actually having existed.

"Where is it?" I struggle to bring myself back to the present, suddenly afraid of a second attack.

"I threw the poor bastard in the river. He won't be bothering us again."

"But the bite, Thomas..." In my artificial memories, the zombie plagues were often spread by bites from the infected. My mind flashes again as images of people trying to care for loved ones already infected grow worse and worse before their eyes. "I'm infected, I—"

Strong hands squeeze my arms and I look up into Thomas's kind eyes. "Imani, the only infection you're going to have is a nasty bacteria from that bloody booger's mouth. We need to get going in case there are guards chasing that nutter or patrolling the woods. You're going to be just fine, you got it? I can get you medicine as soon as we get back across the river."

I nod, feeling a little foolish at my inability to separate the present from the past, truth from the fiction.

"I'm going to get this wet and clean you up, you got it? Then we're on our way. Don't move."

I hear him breaking through the bushes to the water's edge. The sounds of branches scraping against his pants makes me hyperaware. What if another—what did Thomas call them? Not zombie, but wiper—came charging out of the woods at us? I make myself stand up. The ground seems to tilt and swim as I find my footing on the rocky shore and focus on clearing my mind of all foreign memories.

"Don't lose it again." I tell this to myself a few times, but the images keep pushing themselves through the pounding in my head and to the forefront of my mind. It's as if the wiper cracked open the gate to all that information when he tackled me, and now I can't keep it from seeping out.

*Fine then,* I think, *if I can't stop it, I might as well make it useful.*

The image of the institute springs to my mind. I shut my eyes tightly and spin it around as if it were actually on a table in front of me, searching again for anything I might have over-looked. We won't get a second chance at this.

The two main doorways—the southern exit I used to leave the first time, and a northern one mirroring it—are easy to spot. There is a service exit on the west side of the building, but the east is entirely made up of windows facing the trees and moun-tains beyond. We would be spotted in an instant by anyone passing the windows inside.

Walking in the main doors seems ridiculously dangerous, but if the place is as empty as the first time I was there, it might not be a bad option, and is, in fact, my Plan B. Especially con-sidering the fact that the service door seems to lead to the utility rooms and kitchens that are likely crawling with people who would know we don't belong there. But a better option is a large maintenance shaft on the west side. It contains air and water pipes and runs below the building.

"Love, you all right?"

Thomas's voice pulls me back to the deep of night. The moon on his face highlights his concern, bringing him that much closer to my heart.

"Yes," I answer.

He gently reaches up and pulls my right hand away from my face, then uses one finger to push the collar of my shirt and coat away from the bite, leaving my white, round shoulder bear to the night air. The shirt is wet with freezing cold river water and he gently presses it to my wound. It stings and soothes at the same time but the throbbing pain seems to subside.

"You sure you're all right?" He takes my left hand down from my face as well. I didn't even realize it was still pressed to my temple.

I take a deep breath. "Yes. I'm okay. I know where to go and how to get in. We just have to avoid guards—and now wipers, I guess."

Thomas pushes the hair back from my forehead, then he leans in and pressed his lips gently to my skin.

It stirs me deep inside. I look at him, taking in every feature in the moonlight. This is Thomas. He has saved me so many times. He found me in the deepest darkness of my imprisonment and gave me the strength to escape. He came back for me time and time again. He is here now, helping me, tending to me, looking at me *that* way. How could I have ever doubted him?

I reach up and put my hands on his cheeks, pulling him down to my lips and kissing him fully. When we part, he grins.

"What was that for?"

"For everything. For being you. For loving me. For following me, even when I'm completely lost and stupid."

"You are the opposite of stupid. And how could I not come? Man can't live without his heart." He lets the wet shirt rest on my shoulder and pulls me closer with both hands, returning the kiss and then breaking away just as fervently. "As much as I'd like to take your battered and bruised self for a proper snog in the woods right now, we really need to get moving."

"You're right." I feel a tiny bit embarrassed at my sentimentality in the middle of a life-and-death situation. But Thomas shoulders the pack and holds the rifle ready, pointing in front of us with one hand and reaches for me with the other. I secure the cloth on my shoulder and take his hand, letting him pull me up the bank.

Even though the noise of the river is good cover for our own movements, it also covers the sound of anyone approaching. We decide to move from it so that we can't be surprised again. The trees begin to thin out and the shadows from the moonlight loom even more ominous than before.

I don't know if it is my injury or exhaustion from the day's hike and stress, but fatigue starts to weigh heavily on me. I struggle to focus on our location in comparison to my mental maps as I let Thomas pull me along behind him. All the while both of us watch every shadow for movement.

Suddenly, a gleam of white catches my eye. I squeeze

Thomas's hand and pull him to a stop, then motion for him to move to an outcropping of rocks nearby. He changes direction and leads the way, checking each side for lurkers. All is clear, so we hunch down.

I whisper in his ear, "I saw the Institute. It's just ahead, through those trees." He nods and I continue. "We should be near the north entrance. If we move past it to the west, there's a maintenance entrance into a crawl space under the building we can use to travel through the duct work."

He nods again and we begin our slow creep to the west. After a few steps, Thomas squeezes my hand and makes the sign to stop. Then he points to the building, now clearly visible ahead of us over a stand of small scrub.

Two men stand on either side of the large double doors. Each holds a shock rifle at the ready. I look at Thomas, who is studying their position, and then look at the woods beyond and the corner we have to get around.

A branch cracks behind us to our left. Thomas and I both turn to see a figure moving through the trees in the deep shadows, about as far away from us as we are from the guards. Remembering the speed and ferocity of the earlier attack, I slowly sink to my knees, hoping the scrub and shadows will hide me.

Thomas follows me down but instead of crouching motionless on the ground, he starts carefully digging through the loam at his feet. Before I realize what he's doing, he has something in his hand and stands. His arm swings hard and fast, launching a rock into the night.

A loud *thwack* fills the emptiness between the guards and ourselves. The wiper stops his slow march and begins to sniff at the air. A crackle from one of the guard's radios cuts through the night like a knife and in seconds the wiper howls and takes off in their direction.

"Now! Now!" Thomas motions to me frantically as several things happen at once.

The guards come to life, firing into the woods as the wiper bounds forward at an unimaginable speed. Thomas and I race through the scrub, trying to stay out of range and sight of the guards. Howls and screams come from the north entrance. My body aches with the memory of my recent attack, but I keep running as quickly as I can. The skin around my shoulder wound strains in a way that feels like small knives cutting into my skin.

Our wide circle takes us successfully to the west side of the building. The maintenance shaft is ahead of us, but before we can reach it, another wiper races from the trees toward us.

She is young, her blond hair hanging in tangles past her shoulders. She wears the white clothes of the institute and no shoes as she lunges at us, one arm outstretched and her mouth agape.

Thomas is already turning, rifle ready, and he shoots. The once-girl falls to the ground, convulsing in a heap. I take a beat to push through the moment—that could have been one of my classmates—and focus on getting in the building again.

"Well, that did us in," Thomas says. "Hopefully they'll think we're just another guard out here doing our job.

I focus back on the building. The opening is covered by a thin grating to keep animals out. We'll need a tool of some sort to pry it open. It's also smaller than I expected—we'll have to crawl on our stomachs which will slow us down.

I pull Thomas against a large tree and fumble at the pack opening. There is a utility knife at the bottom, but my cold fingers can't feel it among the other items in the dark.

Another howl cuts through the night from the north entrance, followed by more shock rifle fire, then another howl from our left—very close by.

I freeze in fear, but Thomas jerks away from me, pointing the rifle in the direction of the second howl, and fires. A body lurches out of the darkness and falls forward, landing at our feet.

"We gotta hurry, love," Thomas says.

"I know." I dig back in the bag and this time find the knife. "Got it!"

"Let's go." He grabs my hand and pulls me out of the scrub as we sprint to the side of the gleaming white building.

I'm rushing to get us out of the open, worried it will take too long to get the screws off and we'll be spotted, but it's less complicated than I thought. The grate is held in place by small screws that I can easily twist out with the dull edge of my knife. The grate opens silently, and I motion for Thomas to follow me.

"There's another one over here!" a voice calls out from the woods where we left the wiper lying unconscious.

"I thought I heard a shot on this edge, 6785. Were you the one who fired on this guy?" another voice answers as I squeeze deeper into the shaft and watch Thomas pull the grate closed behind us.

"No sir, we were patrolling the east side."

"Then who the hell was out here shooting these droolers besides us?"

"We may have a situation on our hands, sir." A radio cracks through the night as more guards find their way to the spot just beyond our hiding place. "Yes, possible security breach. Leaders may be on the premises. Suggesting full lockdown."

## TWENTY THREE

Once inside, the passage is large enough for us to crawl single file on our hands and knees. In the blueprint in my mind, the building is of simple design. Offices and living quarters house patients and workers along the east side, facing the mountains. The west side features a cafeteria and facilities center with a few rooms marked "Special Purposes." I am certain I don't want to know what Hamen's *special purposes* are. The photograph of my mother seems to have been taken in one of the east rooms, so that is the first place I will go to look for her.

After crawling down a short slope, under the floor of the first level, we continue into the dark of the shaft. Waste water pipes run along one side of the shaft, an annoying obstacle to rub against, but the access must make clogs and other issues easier to deal with for sanitation workers. Most buildings are designed with ease of use and function in mind.

The tunnel leads east, and we follow. The map indicates that the maintenance shaft connects with air shafts that create a grid under the building with access to different rooms through vents in the floor. Dim blue squares of light—security lighting in the hallways above—show that we're coming up on several such air vents.

"There should be a larger access grate to the rooms above on the left at the end. Hopefully we can slip up there and find her," I whisper to Thomas.

Every move we make in haste seems to echo through the entire building, announcing our presence—especially when the rifle knocks gently against the side of the shaft and rings like a gong. We creep slowly, Thomas slinging the rifle strap across his back so it hangs beneath him.

A large tunnel breaks off to our left, then our right, but I continue straight. Dust coats my hands and threatens my nose. I pull my shirt up over my face to filter as much as possible and keep me from sneezing. Eventually we come to the fourth large offshoot. I turn and slide carefully into the slightly smaller shaft, but freeze as I hear voices, faint at first, coming from a small opening just above and in front of me

"—expects us to do with all these droolers running around the woods. Even if we stun them all, we don't have the facilities to lock them up. And I don't know about you, but I didn't sign up to be an executioner."

The footsteps pass over the grate as the two men walk by. All I make out about them are their big boots—security personnel, I think.

A loud sigh. "It's a huge bloody mess, but that's why we're

here. That's why we signed up, Rogers—to fix the mess."

"I know. Have you checked on his girlfriend lately?"

The voices are very faint now, and I strain to hear the other's response. "The old lady in 12? She's completely passed out. Whatever he's giving her has her in another world mentally."

"Okay, good. Let's go…"

Their voices trail off as their footsteps recede to another hallway. I turn to see if Thomas has heard any of the conversation. His face is blanketed in shadows, but I see his head nod. I reach back and find his hand. He squeezes it and I squeeze back. We continue to crawl forward as carefully as possible, hoping for a large vent to appear soon.

Several smaller shafts split off the main one. It is painstaking work and my muscles ache with exhaustion. Several times I want to lay down, close my eyes, catch my breath, but the thought of seeing my mother, the thought that she is alive somewhere above me, so close, keeps me going.

Finally, at the end of the tunnel, a blue square comes into focus, indicating a large grate. I scrape my way quickly there and lay on my back, staring up at it. I hear Thomas take off the pack and rifle before he squeezes up next to me.

"Is this it, lassie?" he whispers.

"I think so. Did you hear what those guards said back there?"

"Not the end. I thought you were waiting so they didn't hear us creeping about down here."

I fill him in on what I'd overheard and take a moment to enjoy the thrill of feeling his body so close to mine, even in this dark and dirty place.

"You think they were talking about your ma?"

"It has to be her. She told me once that she had loved someone before my father. She told me they were old friends. Who else would they call *his girlfriend*?"

"Right. I suppose that's the best we've got," he says. "I'm not sure how I'm going to fit through that hole." He points at the grate above us.

While larger than the previous grates, Thomas is right. I can squeeze through if I take off my coat, but it is clear when Thomas squats beneath the grate that his shoulders are too wide.

"I'll go on my own." I started this trip on my own and having him join me for any part of it was a bonus I hadn't counted on. I'll be perfectly fine finishing on my own—I hope. But I don't move immediately. I take another deep breath and steel myself for the next leg of the journey.

"Imani, love." He speaks even more softly, his lips at my ear. "Your ma's up there, and you're meant to find her. You will be just fine. Have faith, alrighty?"

I smile in the dark and lean in to kiss him one more time.

"If for some reason I can't get back to this vent, I'll try to let you know. Don't wait around here for me for too long."

"If you're not back here in thirty minutes, I'm going to find a bigger vent and blast my way through this place till I find ya."

I chuckle at his ferocity. "How about we just come up with an alternate meeting place?"

"We could do it quiet, I suppose. If you like that kind of stuff." I can barely make out his smile in the dark. "How about the big bridge. We make it there and it's a straight shot to the guards on our side of this fight."

"That is a good plan. Just don't let any wipers sneak up on you," I say.

"I already took out two. I'll be just fine. You try to grab yourself another gun, alrighty?" He touches my face with his hand. "And take care that this don't start bleeding again." He motions to my shoulder.

"Yes, sir." I wrap my good arm around him and kiss him hard and full on the mouth. "Now I need to get out of this coat. My mom is up there somewhere."

I wriggle and try to pull my arms out of the thick fabric. The small space makes it difficult to stretch out and slip it off. The bite on my shoulder aches as I twist and turn. Thomas holds one sleeve and tries to help me get it off without hurting me or making noise, but it's difficult task and takes longer than I hoped. At last, I am free of the warmth and security of the large white coat. There's no more reason to stall.

"Here, take this," Thomas says as he tries to hand me the shock rifle.

"No. You'll need it. I'll try to get something else in here." I push on the grate above me. It isn't secured and rises easily.

I listen for footsteps, then inch myself into a seated position where I can push the grate all the way up and peer into the dim blue hallway above me. It is deserted. I lift the grate the rest of the way off and carefully set it against the wall behind me, then I wiggle my way onto the cold, polished floor.

# TWENTY FOUR

The rooms are numbered on either side in ascending order. Directly across from me is room 2. I take a deep breath and grab my coat from Thomas's outstretched hand then replace the grate on the floor. I wave to Thomas's anxious face looking up through the grate before I set off down the hall.

After room 7, a larger hall bisects my path. I guess this must have been where the guards turned to access the cafeteria. My familiarity with the map of the building makes everything feel oddly familiar, like a faraway dream.

I keep moving forward, my breath growing tighter with each passing room number until suddenly I'm in front of room 12.

I double-check the hall. No one is in sight, and I can't hear any footsteps. I start to turn the knob, then stop myself and peer in the small window. It was a room just like the one I slept in when I was here, only not as large and there is no window. A small person is curled in the bed, unmoving and facing away from me. The dark hair matches my mothers, except for more streaks of gray than I remember. My throat is tight, and my heart feels like a bird. What if it isn't her?

I hesitate for a moment, forbidding myself to look away from the window. The idea of my mother alive has driven me this far, but now that I'm here, the possibility of being wrong overwhelms me. I'm not sure I can take it. I ball my hands into fists and blow the air out of my lungs slowly. I've come too far to back out now, but my hand won't turn the doorknob.

Another breath.

I decide to be direct. If it is her, I will wake her as if we were at home—even though Mother was always the first out of bed and waiting for us in the kitchen with breakfast ready. The only times I remember waking her were when I couldn't sleep.

I will make it one of those times. I see myself as a little girl, moving quietly through the night into my mother's quarters. I turn the knob slowly and push inside, letting the door close behind me before I move to the bed.

It takes two steps before I realize something else is wrong. The curled form is too small, too misshapen to be my mother. I know that I have grown in the time we've been separated, but unless my mother shrank as well, this is not her. I reach out gently to touch the small person wrapped tightly in the sheets.

"Mother?" I whisper.

A hand grabs me from behind, covering my mouth and yanking me backward, away from the bed. Something sharp pokes into my side, and a hot burning sensation swells from the contact, a sharp pain at its center.

"Don't move, don't fight, or I'll stab your liver and you'll bleed out."

I put my hands in the air and let the person pull me into the shadows of the room. The tone is low and threatening, but underneath that is a voice I'd know anywhere and a smell that conjures more memories than any artificial process ever could.

I relax and nod my head in agreement. I put one hand on the hand holding the knife to my side. They are shaking. I put the other hand on the fingers covering my mouth and carefully pry them free. Then I turn to see my mother standing before me—tired and aged, but alive.

"Mother, it's me," I whisper. "Daughter4254." The old identification numbers trickle off my tongue as easily as if I'd never had a name at all. Our eyes meet and recognition lifts the veil of fear from her face.

"Daughter? My daughter?" She drops the knife to the floor with a clatter and takes hold of my face, turning it this way and that as tears well in both of our eyes.

"Yes!" I throw my arms around her and pull her close. No fear. No hesitation. No autoeye watching us. It is the embrace I dreamed of having with my mother for so long. "You're alive. How are you alive?"

"Oh, my daughter." She holds me so tightly it's hard to breathe. But I don't care. She is alive.

"What are you doing? Who is in that bed?" I say trying to

keep my voice low.

She chuckles through her tears. "It's just a wadded-up towel and extra blanket. The guards never come in to check on me."

"But the hair…" I say.

The pressure on my shoulders loosens, and my mother hold me at arm's length, her intelligent eyes examine me. I get a better look at her as well, hardly believing this moment I've craved for so long is real. Her lined face and furrowed brow are framed by hair that has been roughly chopped off at the shoulders. It matches the hair on the bed, silver streaks and all.

"Your hair," I say, touching it gently the ends and remembering all those nights I brushed and braided it for her.

"Necessary sacrifice," she says.

"Why were you hiding?"

"I thought it would be a good way to get a gun and get out of here. I've been trying to escape ever since I found out what Hamen has been doing."

I look at her white night clothes and haggard face. She's been through as much as I have, and I love her more for it. "I can't help you with the gun, but I can help you get out of her." I frown at her clothes and bare feet. "Do you have more clothing? Shoes?"

"I do." She shakes her head and puts her forehead in her palm. "I'm not thinking very clearly. My thoughts are jumbled up and I can't tell which are my own anymore." She pulls a second pair of white pants and shirt out of the dressing table. I look away out of respect as she pulls them on self-consciously.

I know I should wait, we don't have much time, and I need to know. "Mother, did Hamen do something to your head?"

"Yes." She sounds defeated as she pulls on a pair of socks followed by simple leather boots.

I don't have time to press her for information. We have to get out of here and then we can talk about next steps.

"Do you have a coat?" I ask.

"No," she says and looks at me in a way I'm not ready for, like I'm the caregiver and she's the child, relying on me to make everything better. But I will be whoever my mother needs me to be.

"I'll be fine. We don't have far to go." I face her again when the rustling of clothes stops and again, despite the circumstance, feel overwhelming love for the woman before me. My mother, whom I'd buried all those months ago, is standing before me, dressed in white pants and white shirt like an angel from the old days, ready to escape with me. We are finally running away together.

I take off my coat and hand it to her. She smiles and puts it on then picks up the knife from the floor. It's only a butter knife, dull, but still a weapon if used correctly, and certainly better than nothing.

"Let's go." I walk to the door and reach for the handle at the same time I hear the close, heavy tread of boots in the hallway outside.

"Someone's coming." I push her back toward the bathroom and we crowd behind the door. Our breathing, labored from the scare, synchronizes as we listen.

The blue light spilling under the door from the hallway dims for a moment then returns to normal intensity.

"It's just a spot check. He'll move on around the building and be back in forty minutes," my mother whispers.

I nod and move back to the door, careful to watch for movement and to listen for any sounds on the other side. All is still.

"I have a friend waiting for us in the maintenance shaft at the end of the hallway. If we can get to him, we can slip outside, and they'll never see us."

"Right," she says.

I try the door again, more gingerly this time. I don't hear anything, so I peer around the corner. Nothing. I motion for Mother to follow me and make my way into the hall.

We move as quickly and quietly as possible, slipping along the wall toward the square on the floor at the other end.

I slow as we approach the adjoining hallway, listening for any indication of someone approaching. Just a few more steps and I'll be with Thomas and my mother, and we can take a minute to figure out how to get out of here.

Just as I'm about to look around the corner of the hallway, the sound of an opening door followed by bright yellow light comes from the cross hallway. My mother cowers behind me as footsteps approach. Panicking, I look at the vent. We could run for it, but then they'd know we were here, and they'd know how to trap us. Maybe the person will just walk by as we stand frozen at the corner of our hall—

A man in a white coat turns the corner and walks right into me. I tumble to the ground but scramble up again so fast I feel like I bounced. I pull my mother up from where she fell and push her back in the direction we came from, shouting, "Run!"

"Hey! What are you—"

The man seems more surprised than we are, but I don't plan on sticking around to explain to him why we're sneaking around the hallway at night. Mother and I are already halfway back to her room when I hear the man yell, "Wait! You're mountain people, aren't you? Wait!"

The man following us has a short, stocky frame—no match for our panicked wiry bodies, but he does his best to keep up.

Mother matches me stride for stride, though her breathing is much more labored. The hall is longer than I remembered, and we are probably waking up every person in the building as we dash for our escape, but we don't have any other choice.

I hear a strained cry from behind us. "Wait for me!"

We turn a couple of corners into new passages. It's not easy, but I've pulled the plans up in my head again and am focusing on the exits. Finally, we reach the hall to the southern exit. Through the tiny windows in the double doors that lead outside at the end of the hall, I can see the heads of two guards in white hats. I slow down. The man following us is definitely not a guard, but that doesn't make him a friend. Lights flood the door windows from outside—truck headlights. I only hope Thomas heard my cry and got out of the building in time to meet us by the bridge.

"Where should we go?" Mother asks as I slow to assess the situation. Part of me still hopes she will take charge, as she always did when I was a small one. But another part of me knows she can't. This is my plan, my domain. I have to get us both out of here.

I stretch my mind, trying to find the blueprint, trying to find another way out, but the little man behind us wails again, breaking my concentration.

"Please, stop. Listen to me." His face is dark red, and he is completely out of breath as he shuffles closer. "You can't go out there. It's crawling with Hamen's men. I know who you are. He'll throw you in a truck and take you into the city before you can shake a shock rifle at him. If you want to get out of here, you've got to take me with you."

He stops out of reach, but I still hold the knife out at him, warning him not to come closer. I look at the wheezing man with incredulity. "No."

"You don't have a choice. I know how to get out of here. There's a service door by the kitchens that leads to the woods."

I snort. "You mean the woods full of wipers waiting to eat our heads off our bodies?" My shoulder is aching now that we're standing still after the sprint.

He looks at me blankly. "Is it that bad already?"

"Yes." I pull at the collar of my shirt to show him my bruised and bloody skin. Fresh blood runs from cracks in the clotted wound.

"Oh, Daughter!" Mother touches my forearm gently, expression aghast at the injury. "What happened?"

"I'll explain later." I purse my lips, looking between the exit and the man. Then I decide, and I take my mother's hand to give it a comforting squeeze. "For now, I think I know what we can do. Just run as fast as you can, okay?"

"Okay," she says, looking resolute and ready.

While I'm distracted, the doctor comes closer, and puts a hand on my forearm. "I'm slow but I can help. I'm Dr. Bower. Head of research and development."

His title piques my interest, but I'm already shaking him off, moving toward the double doors. There are bigger issues at the moment than picking Dr. Bower's brain. "Fine, but you have to keep up."

A barrage of shots outside, followed by a banging, make me freeze. Howls fill the air, interrupted by more shots. The heads of the guards disappear, heading toward a threat I can't see. Dr. Bower whimpers.

I pause by the window in the right door, wanting to get as much information about the situation outside. Several large trucks are parked in the yard with engines running and headlights on. Wipers are everywhere, running in and out of the headlights with manic speed. About seven guards form a loose semi-circle in front of the doors, shock rifles blasting nonstop. More guards are around the trucks, chasing wipers or taking cover. Between two guards, I see one down, a wiper gnawing on his ankle while the guard kicks it in the head with a steel-toed boot.

"Why are there suddenly so many wipers? Where are they all coming from?" I ask.

"We don't know. We started to get reports that they were going missing from their assignments and then they began showing up in the woods around the institute." Dr. Bower's voice is quiet and terrified.

As if a retreat has been called, those guarding the entrance suddenly turn back toward the double doors. They are shouting something, but I can't tell what.

I ask Mother, "Can you drive a truck?"

She nods at me, eyes wide and scared.

I grab her hand and push the door open, ready to sprint out, but the guards have already reached us and they force their way past us.

"Hold the door!" one at the back screams. "It's locked from the inside. Hold the door!"

"Don't let any of them inside!" Another guard shoves his way in past Mother, and I hold on to her arm to help her stay standing.

Then I strongarm our way out into the fray.

"Where are you going?" the guard yells after us. Then the doors swing shut, and his voice is cut off.

We dodge guards and wipers as we run the few steps to the closest open-top truck. Luckily there seems to be enough fallen guards to distract the wipers, and I don't let myself look at the men being devoured.

*I can't help them without endangering her,* I tell myself.

We reach the truck and I climb in the passenger's side. There are no doors and the back is open behind the bench seat, allowing for hauling large cargo or several people at once. It might not provide much cover, but least it is faster than these creatures. I search the back and under the seats for a weapon. My hand lands on the cold barrel of a shock rifle under the rear seat, and I pull it out and check the battery—one quarter charge remaining. Good for a couple shots. Mother climbs into the driver's seat and starts to shove pedals and push buttons until the machine lurches to a start.

"Wait!" Dr. Bower is ten feet from the truck, a wiper with a bloody mouth just behind him. Another wiper scrabbles at my door. I swing it open into its face, and it collapses. I lower the window enough to aim at the wiper grabbing Dr. Bower's white jacket from behind. But it's just as likely I'll hit the doctor as the wiper.

"Take off your coat and jump in!" I yell, still aiming at the wiper. "When he gets in, Mother, head toward the mountains."

"But there's no road."

"Just drive that way and don't hit any rocks or trees."

The doctor and his attacker are close enough that I can clearly see the wiper, a woman with dark eyes hungry for Dr. Bower's soft white skin. With a wriggle, he does as I instruct, and the creature slips behind, giving me room to blast it.

Dr. Bower jumps in the back seat and Mother stomps down on the accelerator. The truck lurches forward, rocking me into the seat back. Dr. Bower squeals as his door slams shut with the momentum of the truck. It's a strange sound coming from a grown man. As she maneuvers her way through the rest of the skirmish, we approach the last truck, farthest from the doors of the institute. Both doors open as we get closer, and two guards bail out—followed by Hamen.

Mother doesn't notice him, but I make eye contact through my open window. He shouts at a guard, gesturing wildly. The guard turns in our direction and takes aim, firing. Only one shot hits the back of the truck before a wiper leaps from the dark and tackles him. Trees cut off my line of view just after Hamen takes the man's dropped rifle and shoots the wiper in the face.

# TWENTY FIVE

**M**other drives over the rough forest floor like a born bushwhacker. She slaloms trees and bounces over rocks, forcing the four wheels to spin as fast as they possibly can. Dr. Bower lurches around the back seat like a ball, and I hold onto a handrail with one hand and the shock rifle with the other.

A wiper appears, running at an inhuman speed to match our pace. He reaches out for Mother, who wails and swerves away.

"Steady! I'll get him."

She rights our course, allowing the wiper to catch up again, but I take aim behind her seat and shoot him in the chest.

"Hey!" Dr. Bower shrieks. "That is too close! The energy from the rifle could hit any of us at this proximity."

I ignore him and watch for more attackers.

The trees and brush are getting thicker.

"I don't think I can drive much farther," Mother calls over the whine of the engine.

"There's a bridge ahead. Just a few more yards. Go as far as you can—"

The truck lurches to a stop and we are thrown violently forward, then back. The engine roars and the front end comes off the ground, tires spinning wildly.

"What on earth?" Dr. Bower says.

"There must be something in the bush. We're high centered." Mother's answer is surprisingly calm.

There's no time to waste. "We've got to run. I'll lead the way with the gun," I say, gesturing for them to get out.

Once the engine is shut off, I can hear the rush of the river, as well as the distant whine of another truck—Hamen.

I begin to run, beckoning to my mother and the doctor. "Come on. They're right behind us."

We race through the brush and trees. The sound of the river grows louder, but a glance back reveals two beams of light getting closer. Hamen is gaining. At least we seem to be avoiding wipers, but I'm not sure how long our luck will hold.

The trees thin and then end. The river is there, roaring through the ravine in front of us. The noise, although deafening, is a relief. I scan the banks and sight the solid cement pillars of the bridge a hundred yards to our left.

"This way!" I shout and pull on Mother's arm as I move in the direction of the pillars. Dr. Bower is behind us, gasping erratically.

Suddenly I feel Mother jerk the opposite way. I look back— into the eyes of the wiper who has hold of her other arm. He is too close to shoot, and I can't aim with one arm, so I swing the rifle as hard as I can, hitting him in the head with the barrel. It stuns him long enough for Mother to get away. She slips behind me and I point the shock rifle at the man just as he regains his balance and bares his teeth at me. I pull the trigger. A burst of light shoots from the barrel but disappears before it reaches his chest. The man roars and charges forward. I slam the gun into the wiper's face again, and this time I feel his jaw dislocate with a wet *crack* before he collapses.

"What happened?" Mother cries as I pull us both toward the bridge.

"Out of power." I keep the gun, though. It's proved useful as a club.

Mother is ahead of me, and Dr. Bower got ahead of us in the scuffle, already making his way across the dark bridge over the moonlit water. The river's deafening roar makes it impossible to know if wipers are approaching, and I expect bony fingers on my own clothing any moment. Instead, the sound of the second truck and shock rifle blasts cut through the night.

Mother runs up the steps and starts across the bridge. Dr. Bower pauses halfway across and starts yelling something at me. I ignore him. I have to find Thomas. I scan the rocks and bushes around bridge's head frantically. Two wipers appear out of the woods to my right and run toward me. The rifle blasts of Hamen's soldiers are getting closer.

And then I see him.

Thomas stands just inside the tree line to my right, swinging the rifle in both hands like a long sword to fight off three wipers. One wiper scratches his face before being bludgeoned away.

I sprint to his side, thinking only of protecting this boy who has stuck with me through everything. When I'm within striking distance, I hold the gun by its barrel and swing with all my might at the closest wiper's head. It crumples to the ground, leaving one each for us to contend with.

"Hello, love!" Thomas cries, blood dripping down his cheek. "Fine night for a fight, eh?"

I swing at another wiper, but it dodges, and I only deliver a glancing blow to his shoulder.

"Just get to the bridge!" I shout back at him.

We maneuver around so they are no longer between us and freedom, but the wipers have wised up and dodge our blows. We progress backward slowly, constantly warding off sharp nails and teeth.

I risk a glance back and see Dr. Bower in the center of the bridge, watching us struggle. Mother is shouting at us as well but isn't leaving the bridge to help. Her words are garbled, but a few more steps and I catch traces

"Wipers won't cross… water."

One more step, and mother's words become clear: the wipers don't like water. They won't cross the bridge.

At the same moment, Thomas and I turn from the wipers we had been battering and sprint to the bridge. Bony fingers claw at my back and hair for a terrifying instant but slip away as I step over the threshold of stone and onto the deep brown timbers spanning the river.

Mother is there, embracing me before we start our run again. Just because wipers won't cross the bridge doesn't mean the guards—and their shock blasts—won't.

"I'm going to sprint ahead to the guard house." Thomas squeezes my hand and is off before I can answer.

"Come on, Mother. Not much farther now." I take her hand and lead her toward the opposite side of the bank as fast as I think she can go. We are steps away from safety, and my heart lightens knowing all the people I love will be safe soon.

More shots sound behind us. Lights flash through the air, casting a shadow on the narrow wood before me. Mother's hand spasms then jerks out of mine, and I turn in time to see her fall.

I can't see where she's been shot, but there's no time to check. I grab her arms and drag her behind me, stumbling and struggling until other hands are there, helping me lift her. I look up, ready to fight, when I recognize the green coats and hoods. They are mountain folk. With a sob, I let them lift Mother as if she weighs nothing and jog with her off the bridge. Thomas slides around them and takes my hand. More shots are fired around us.

"Come on, Imani. Run! We've got to go!"

I follow his lead, stumbling as I stare at Mother's limp form in the arms of the mountain guards instead of the planks beneath my feet.

We're stepping onto the stone threshold of the opposite end of the bridge when a deafening explosion fills the air with light and sound, and then all is black.

# TWENTY
# SIX

The smell of something cooking on wood smoke tickles at my nose and pulls me from my deep sleep. Crisp, cool air fills my lungs as my mind slowly wakes. My head throbs and the shoulder the wiper bit aches and burns. I open my eyes to a dull glow on canvas walls. A scratchy blanket rubs my chin.

The small space is filled with cots and blankets and various clothing items folded in neat piles atop two large trunks. A black barrel stove stands in one corner. Heat from red coals radiates through the vent holes, and a pot simmers on top. A cot within arm's reach of mine holds the form of my mother, chest rising and falling with each breath.

I blink away the tears that suddenly flood my eyes. She is here. She is alive. We are together. I reach out my hand to touch her arm, to make sure this moment is real. Her soft skin is just as I remembered it as a child—warm, smooth, and covered in the smallest of brown hairs.

Beyond my mother, the tent flap parts and Thomas walks in, smiling broadly despite a slight limp. His face is bandaged on the left side. He takes off his coat, tossing it on another cot, and sits beside me, bending close to scoop me into his arms and kiss my cheek.

"Ya did it, lass. You got her," he whispers.

"Is she well? They shot her on the bridge." I look at her peaceful face one more time.

"She's right as rain. Surprised they hit her after all that wiper whacking and with how far off you two were. We're going to do some hunting to see if they've modified their weapons."

The rest of last night comes back to me in a rush. "What was that explosion? Is anyone else hurt?" I rest a gentle hand on top of his bandaged face.

"Nothin' that won't heal quick. Our folk have been planning on taking the bridge out for a while. When news came that the two of us had prolly gone to raid the Institute, they were ready for anything. When I showed up screaming like a fool about the guards and wipers coming, I guess they got a little trigger happy and fired her up a bit early. Are you feeling all right? You've had a few nasty bumps to the head in the past couple weeks."

I take a deep breath, assessing what hurts. "I'm sore, and my head hurts, but I'm all right. Where are we?"

"We're still at the bridge base camp."

I sit up a bit in surprise, afraid of being so close to the Institute and all the wipers. "Won't Hamen and his men be coming after us?"

"No. There's a bit of a standoff going on. Hamen's men pulled back after we blew the bridge. I suppose they are worried that we've got the whole east bank booby trapped." Thomas chuckles. "Not a bad idea, actually."

I lie back on my pillow and take another deep breath. He reaches over carefully and pushes my loose shirt away from my throbbing shoulder.

"How's this feeling?"

"Not too bad," I whisper back. "My head hurts worse, and my whole body feels like one of those trucks ran me down."

"Well then. I might just have to take care of your whole body." He grins wickedly and leans in to kiss me. His stubble burns my cheeks and chin in a wonderful way.

"I'm not dead, you know," my mom says from her cot.

Thomas jerks up and we both look in my mother's direction, guilt covering our faces. She's on her side, eyes wide, facing us.

"Don't let me stop you. Just wanted you to know I am here and breathing," she says, face serious.

"Mother!" I move to sit up, but pain shoots through my head like a shock rifle, and I lie back with a groan.

"Easy, Daughter. There will be plenty of time for jumping up later. Are you feeling better?"

"Yes. I'm going to be fine. It's just my head."

"I think you should properly introduce me then." She motions to Thomas.

"Oh, right. Mother, this is Thomas. Thomas, this is my mother," I say.

Thomas reaches out a hand in the traditional fashion, following the Leader's protocol. "It's a pleasure to finally meet Imani's amazing mother."

Mother takes his hand and smiles. Then she looks at me. "Imani?"

"Yes." I smile back. "Thomas gave me the name when we met in prison."

"I like it." She reaches out and takes my hand too. "Imani suits you."

a sneak peek at

# BOOK THREE

in the *Daughter 4254* series

When I finally make it outside the tent with Thomas's help, the view is grim. Men and women wipers in dirty, torn uniforms stumble along the opposite edge of the small canyon carved by the river. Occasionally one slips and falls, sliding on the rocky surface into the river below. If they survive, they try to pull themselves back up, desperate to get away from the rush of the swift flowing water. They are mindless wanderers, stripped of their personalities and any other sign of humanity. The remains of the bridge hang in black tatters. The flames on our side are extinguished. Hamen's men on the other side are gone. There is nothing left to do but plan our next move.

"Come away from there, love." Thomas takes me by the arm and pulls me gently back to camp.

The reconnaissance team is no longer hiding. They have pitched a little tent city in the open clearing by the bridge cabin. Fires burn in the center of the circle of dwellings and smoke plumes from each stove pipe poking from the tents. Hamen and his resistance know we are here. The Leaders know we are here. Thomas and I have defied both them, and I'm not sure what they are going to do about it.

"I don't understand how Hamen could have done all of this and not care," I say as I follow him.

"Done all of what?" Thomas asked.

"Ruined all of those people and left them in the mountains to die. They don't have any way of protecting themselves or feeding—"

"Actually, they do quite nicely feeding themselves on anything they can catch," he cuts in, looking pointedly at my bandaged shoulder.

"That's gross. Stop it."

He laughs and takes my hand. "There's going to be a meeting in a bit here. We need to decide if we're heading back to the mines or not."

Thomas and I walk back into the camp, openly holding hands. I don't feel like I have to hide anything anymore. I am too tired to worry about things like that. I guess he feels the same way. A few of his people give us strange looks, perhaps knowing of his almost engagement to Alice. Or maybe there is some rule against hand holding. Either way, I don't care.

We stop in front of my tent. "How about you go check on your mother and meet me at the main campfire in a few minutes?" He smiles and squeezes my hand before he lets it go.

My mother. It feels so strange to say the words. She has been dead for so long, and now she is back. The word "ghost" pops into my mind, a spirit come back from the dead to haunt the living. They are opaque and float around making scary noises and throwing things. But as I lift the flap to the tent, I see my mother—real, solid, smiling.

"Good morning," she says.

Even though I saw her not that long ago, I can't help my-self—I walk up to her and embrace her. She still has the smell of Hamen's facility about her, but there is also the underlying smell I know so well. It only belonged to her. I let it fill my mind and mingle with the fresh cool air of the pines and wood smoke and feel truly, deeply happy for the first time in years. I don't want to let her go, and I can tell she doesn't want to release me either. Eventually, I sit beside her and hold her hand.

"They are having a camp-wide meeting in a few minutes," I say.

"I figured they couldn't stay here on the side of the mountain for much longer. Food is scarce with this many," she replies.

Nothing has changed. Mother was always worried about feeding everyone in our community back at home, and now she is starting up with complete strangers in the middle of a dire situation.

"Do you have any idea what they are going to do with me?" she asks.

"I don't. They have been fairly kind to me. I haven't had much trouble." Joe's late-night offer in the kitchen and Adelaide's animosity flash through my mind, but I push all that aside. I don't want to burden her with too much information yet. "They'll be trying to decide what to do with me as well. Not many of the mountain people are happy about me wandering into their lives and bringing two regimes down on them."

She nods and stands stiffly. "Can't blame them for that, I suppose. Let's head out there." She wraps the blanket from her cot around her shoulders. Our hasty escape didn't give us time to raid the Institutes cold weather gear. She still has on the white sleeping clothes and soft cotton shoes given to her in Hamen's facility.

"I'll see if I can find you some socks and boots. It's still cold outside. There is snow on the ground in places." I look lamely around the small tent for something else she can wear.

"I'll be all right. I don't need anything more than what I have now."

We both turn at the thumping on the tent pole nearest the entrance, followed by the cheery greeting, "Hello, ladies. Are you both set?"

I pull back the flap and let my mother walk between Thomas and I into the cold, sunny air. Thomas shows her the way, and I follow, glancing only briefly behind me at the distant shore where movement catches my eye.

The main fire at the center of camp is stoked and feels warm and welcoming. Several men I don't know sit on stumps and rocks at the edge of the small clearing. Most are holding shock rifles and are dressed to blend in with the brush and trees. Dr. Bowman stands off to one side, looking awkward in his white Institute clothing and an over-sized coat. He holds a mug of something steaming and my mouth begins to water.

A man approaches us carrying a coat. "We retrieved this from our supplies. Here." He offers it to Mother, who takes it gladly.

"Thank you," she says as Thomas takes her blanket, and she slips the coat on and zips it up.

The man lingers longer than I expected, smiling at her. He's about her age. His black hair is flecked with white and gray strands over his ears—salt and pepper, my artificial memory tells me. Mother smiles back at him. It is a strange inter-change—quick, but I catch it.

"We have soup cooking and lots to talk about," he says. Then he offers her his arm. She takes it and steps ahead of us.

I look at Thomas who looks back at me, eyebrows raised. We both follow them into the gathering. I lean in and whispered. "Do you have any idea what the plan is? For us?"

"I don't," he whispers back. "But don't fret your head. It's not going to be anything bad. I'll make sure of it."

"But Thomas, they lied to you about finding my mother and didn't include you or your mother in the meeting where they bullied me into being their walking encyclopedia. Plus, I think Joe has other plans…" I don't want to remember, let alone talk about the night with Joe in the kitchens.

"They can be as shady as they like, I still have friends and I know things just as well as they do." He smiles at me, his eyes searching my face for trust and understanding.

"Just don't hold anything back. I need to know everything too. We need to do this together," I say. Our earlier miscommunications had ended with me shooting Thomas in the chest. It made me sick to think about, and I squeezed his hand.

"You got it."

Thomas leads me to where Mother has settled on a stump near the fire, and I sit on one beside her. She is sipping broth from a tin can, as are many of the men and women around us. Thomas brings me my own tin and sits beside me. The broth inside fills me with a delicious warmth as I sip and study the people around me.

The salt-and-pepper man stands to one side of a taller, darker man with a stern face. He holds his gun like he means to use it at any moment. His feet are spread shoulder width apart and he looks from face to face as he speaks.

"This is what remains of our outpost team. As far as we have been able to tell, the Blue Spider rebels have either fled their side of the shore or are holed up in the Institute. Dr. Bowman," he nods to the nervous man, "has offered to fill us in on any and all intelligence he is privy to in exchange for asylum. We have agreed to this arrangement with certain restrictions. He will not possess a weapon, he will be accompanied at all times, and he will go on the record and speak to the council at the mines when we return. The question now is which of us should go back and which should we keep at the outpost."

He turns his gaze to my mother and me. "Also, there is the matter of our new female companions. What do you have to say for yourselves?"

I look at my mother. Before either of us can speak, Thomas answers for us.

"They also have information on Hamen and the Leaders we can use. I propose we return them to the mines as well and let them speak to the council."

"That one's already reported and a fat lot of good it did us," one of the women to my right says as she points at me.

"Silence," the serious man says. "I'm aware of the history. Thomas, they will speak for themselves."

I don't hesitate. "My mother and I would like to request asylum."

"I'm not sure that will be possible given the fact that you violated your original agreement."

"There were extenuating circumstances." I can be just as serious.

"And would you like to report these *circumstances* to us now?" he asks.

"I was threatened by Hamen and by those inside your organization. I felt it best to take matters into my own hands and get my mother out of the Institute."

"What manner of threats did you receive?"

I looked at Thomas, who clearly doesn't know what I am talking about. I'm not sure I want him to know.

"Hamen was going to kill my mother if I didn't return. The council wasn't going to let me leave and had no plan to free her. They lied to me."

"And do you have proof of these lies?" He is defensive, like he doesn't believe me.

"I do. The guards that were sent to retrieve her never left the mines."

A murmur filters through the group.

"Enough," the man says. "We will deal with this in front of the council. We have no quarrel, that I've been informed of, with your mother. She may accompany the group heading back to the mines, but only temporarily, until her asylum has been approved. Unlike some," he nodded toward the far side of the river where the wipers staggered, "we do not leave our brothers and sisters to wander the wilderness helpless and alone."

I look at my mother, temporary relief filling my chest.

"Captain, what do we do about the wipers?" the salt-and-pepper man asks.

"There is nothing we can do. We man the guard house and keep our eyes on them. I'm not sure what the next few days will bring. Dr. Bowman, would you care to fill us in on the status of your mindless army over there?"

"They aren't mine," he shoots back quickly. His voice is stronger than his paleness would suggest. "I was recruited to work with Hamen after he heard me complaining about the state of the government and the choices the Leaders were making in regard to MindWipe science. I wanted access to ancient medical records and information. It was denied, of course, and that's when Hamen approached me. His plan to reinstate all of the old knowledge was too tempting to let go, so I joined him. It was about a year into the project that we started seeing issues. The subjects that had been retained for studies began to regress mentally. I felt we should issue alerts for communities where other subjects were serving, in case they were experiencing the same regressions, but Hamen said no."

In the brief shocked silence after this declaration, I ask, "You knew about this all along? Hamen knew and didn't stop the program?"

"We were only starting to understand when—" He is cut off by the captain.

"What I want to know is where did all of these sodding wipers come from? All the sudden your side of the shore is crawling with them when this entire region was deserted before."

"Hamen kept a facility underground for test subjects that needed further research. Some had escaped prior to that, but last night the security systems were disabled and they were able to escape."

Thomas coughs and digs his toe the dirt. I look up at him from my stump. He avoids my gaze and puts a hand on my shoulder.

"What did you do?" I whisper.

He shakes his head and nods back to the conversation in front of us.

"Bowman, I only want to know one more thing before we haul you up to the council. Why did you defect now?"

"Hamen is a madman. I wish I'd known it before, but I'm certain now, and I knew you were my last hope. My community thinks I'm dead. I have no identity. If I slip back into Leader society, they will lock me up once they find out I'm a traitor and I'll end up getting the wipe as well. There is no way I want Hamen to touch my mind. He can't be trusted. He's destroying good people. I'd rather take my chances with you than risk that."

My mother sits with her head in her hands. I feel sick to my stomach as all of this information begins to shift into place. There is only one piece of the puzzle I don't have yet.

"How long?" I ask.

"How long what?" Bowman says.

"How long after Hamen messes with subjects before they turn into wipers?"

Bowman pursed his lips. "Every subject was different, but most in our program were within six months. I'm not sure about the ones out in the community. MindWipe failures aren't something the Leaders would publicize."

"Six months?" My throat feels tight and my stomach turns over. I suddenly regret the soup I've just eaten.

"Give or take," he says, completely oblivious to what his words mean to me.

Thomas squeezes my shoulder again and says, "Yah, but those were the ones he wiped. What about the ones he added to?"

Bowman shrugged. "I was not a part of those experiments. They were just beginning when I arrived, but I believe the results were similar."

The meeting continues around us, but all I hear is a roaring in my ears. *Six months.*

Thomas's hand in mine refocuses me. "Hey, lass." He leans over and whispers in my ear, "There's nothing to be afraid of."

I want to believe him. But there are so many things he doesn't know. So many things we can't control.

The meeting winds up and assignments are made. I haven't heard a single word. I turn to my mother.

"Mother?" I say.

She looks at me and smiles. "It's so good to hear that name again."

I want to ask her about dates—how long ago did he wipe her mind, did he implant anything, does she think we're in danger—but I can't start my sentence.

"Let's go get packed up," she says. "I can't wait to meet these mountain folk you've been dreaming about for so long."

"You'll love them," Thomas says.

"I'm sure I will." She smiles at him and takes my half-finished mug of soup from me. "Are you sure you don't want to finish this?"

"I'm fine," I lie. My stomach feels like a pit of acid. I can't eat another bite.

# ACKNOWLEDGEMENTS

First, thank you to the Wattpad community who read and commented on the rough draft of this novel as I wrote it. Second, thank you to my family for letting me be a writer. Super huge thanks to my editor, Olivia. She's also great at adjusting deadlines. Thank you to Lori Kilkelly, my kickbutt agent, everyone who ever beta read this crazy project (there were a lot of you sweet souls), and to Emma, for believing in me and Imani.

# Leigh Statham

Leigh Statham was raised in the wilds of rural Idaho but found her heart in New York City. She now resides in North Carolina and has an MFA in Young Adult literature from Converse College where she serves as the Managing Fiction Editor at *South 85 Journal*. She is the winner of the 2018 James Applewhite Poetry prize honorable mention and *Southeast Review* 2016 Narrative Nonfiction prize.

She is the author of the Perilous Journey of the Not-So-Innocuous Girl series. Her essays, poetry, and short stories can be found in the *Remington Review*, *Southeast Review*, *North Carolina Literary Review*, and several anthologies.

## Follow Leigh Statham on

leighstatham.com

#D4254 | #ImaniUnraveled

CPSIA information can be obtained
at www.ICGtesting.com
Printed in the USA
BVHW030828050219
539513BV00001B/52/P

9 781945 654251